BOOKS BY KEELY BROOKE KEITH

UNCHARTED

The Land Uncharted
Uncharted Redemption
Uncharted Inheritance
Christmas with the Colburns
Uncharted Hope
Uncharted Journey
Uncharted Destiny
Uncharted Promises
Uncharted Freedom
Uncharted Courage

UNCHARTED BEGINNINGS

Aboard Providence
Above Rubies
All Things Beautiful

Uncharted Redemption

KEELY BROOKE KEITH

Edenbrooke
Press

Edenbrooke Press
Nashville, Tennessee

Uncharted Redemption

Printed in the United States of America

ISBN-13: 978-0692298626
ISBN-10: 0692298622

Library of Congress Control Number: 2014922468
Edenbrooke Press, Nashville, TN

Cover designed by Najla Qamber Designs
Edited by Dena Pruitt
Interior design by Edenbrooke Press
Author photo courtesy of Frank Auer

For every girl who ever felt ruined

CHAPTER ONE

L evi Colburn hammered a nail into the frame of a house that would end seven generations of family tradition. He straightened his back and surveyed the four completed wall frames—all of which lay flat on the ground, begging to be raised. Ready to see the frame of his house upright, he tied a rope to the top of each wall. Wiping the sweat from his forehead, he glanced at the angle of the morning sun and then at the road through the clearing at the front of his property. Everett was late.

Levi dropped his hammer onto the building site's leveled ground and stared at the road. He needed Everett's help to raise the frame but loathed the thought of waiting any longer. As he paced the subfloor, he calculated the logistics of completing the task by himself. If he could get the frame up and the roof on, he could be sleeping in the small house in a matter of days.

He walked across his cleared property to the road to look for Everett. Stagnant air left the usually rustling gray leaf trees still. Without a steady ocean breeze, he found the gray leaf's pleasant but medicinal aroma potent. He intended to complete his house before the end of the austral summer, so he had to continue the job with or without help—or a breeze. After a quick glance toward the Fosters' sheep farm, he decided Everett was either too busy or had simply forgotten his promise to help lift the heavy frames. Either way, Levi couldn't wait another day.

The Fosters' dog scampered down from its place on the front steps of their farmhouse and bounded to Levi with its tail wagging. He ignored the dog's giddy greeting and looked down the road toward the village of Good Springs. After confirming his solitude, he turned and walked back to the wall frames on his property.

He surveyed the pieces that would soon form the skeleton of his long-awaited home. Then he looked at the muddy dog licking his boots. "Well, Shep, if I'm meant to live here alone, I can raise the frame alone." The dog stopped following him and whimpered. He took it as a challenge and marched toward the wall frames. Determined to see his house built, he snatched his hammer from the dust and slipped it through his belt loop. He drew two long planks from a high stack of lumber and carried the wood to the first wall. With a row of nails trapped between his lips, he bent to the grounded frame and hammered the support boards into place.

Confident in his bodily strength, he slid his hands into a pair of leather work gloves and gathered the ropes attached to the top of the wall's frame. He wrapped the left rope around his left hand and the right rope around his right hand. Gripping the ropes, he walked backward in incremental steps and pulled with steady force until the wall was upright. He moved quickly to the center of the skeletal wall and drove nails through the frame and into the subfloor below. Then he reinforced the wall from the other side.

His pride at conquering the first wall added a slight swagger to his gait as he walked to the lumber stack. He repeated the process on the opposite wall of his new home. While raising the second wall, the muscles in his shoulders burned in protest of such a great demand. He stopped his work after securely bolstering the second wall and stretched his neck deep to one side and then to the other.

As he caught his breath through parted lips, he studied the long wall that would be the back of his house. He mentally gauged its weight while he drew a handkerchief from his trouser pocket. Wiping his face, he looked at the road again and hoped to see Everett Foster.

Still alone—and still determined—Levi secured four pieces of support lumber to the long wall. With his back to the road, he wrapped the ropes around his gloved hands. He imagined the house's frame complete and conjured every ounce of strength he could to lift the wall from the ground. His muscles strained and trembled as the wall inched away from the dirt. The ropes squeezed tighter around his hands. The wall barely climbed halfway to an upright position when the rope in his right hand snapped. The skewed weight on the other rope jerked it from his hand, pulling the glove off and ripping a chunk of his palm along with it.

He clutched his torn hand to his chest and blew out a growl of pain. The wall frame bounced once when it hit the ground and sent dirt flying into the air. Blood flowed from his hand and dripped between his fingers. He pulled his shirt over his head and wrapped it around his bloody hand. The cloth of the shirt immediately absorbed the warm sticky blood. He stepped off the subfloor and moved toward the road; his stiff breath was stunted by the shock of searing pain.

As he approached the clearing, he saw Mandy Foster standing on the road in front of his property. Shep raced to her, but she didn't look at the dog. Her mouth gaped and her green eyes protruded as she stared at his blood-soaked bandage. "Levi!"

Mandy was the last person Levi wanted to see in his current condition. He groaned and wondered if she had witnessed the actions that led to the injury, but he was too preoccupied with physical pain to feel embarrassment. No doubt the barbed blanket of humiliation would be waiting to cover him when the pain subsided.

Mandy ran and met him before he reached the road. "What happened to you?"

He ignored her question, wanting her to go away as much as he wanted her to come closer. He stopped walking and peeled the fabric back from his hand to wrap it tighter. She touched his arm as she looked at his wounded palm. "You have to go to Lydia."

"It's just the skin."

"No, your flesh is torn. You need stitches."

She was right, but he wouldn't admit it aloud. He struggled with the shirt he was using as a bandage and moaned at the thought of going to his sister for help, even if she were the village's only doctor. Though the pain's grip was beginning to lessen, the intense throb of his torn hand made his pulse ring in his ears. He sucked in a breath to speak. "No. If my father sees me wounded from working on the house alone, I will never hear the end of it."

"Lydia is probably in her cottage. Your father may not see you go to her." She reached for the bloodied shirt then rewrapped his hand with enough pressure to slow the trickle of blood. He wondered if the blood bothered her and watched her face. She glanced at his bare chest then up at his eyes. Her finely arched brows pulled together. "How did this happen? You weren't raising the walls alone, were you?"

He wasn't sure which was worse: ripping his hand open or being questioned by the coquette who once rejected him. He snapped his wounded hand away from her and trudged down the road toward the village. When she caught up and walked beside him, he sighed audibly. "I don't need a chaperone."

Her long red curls bounced as she sauntered down the gravel road beside him. "If you lose any more blood, you will need a stretcher."

He wanted to divert her attention away from his wounded state. He noticed the flecks of wood shavings that clung to the ends of her hair. "What brought you out of your workshop?"

She pointed her proud chin toward the village. "I heard the groans of a pitifully wounded carpenter and decided to escort him to the doctor." She smiled and assumed a mock cuteness that made him want to pull her hair and run away like he did when they were children. He didn't know how to tell her he loved her then, and wouldn't dare tell her now. Not again.

He glanced at his throbbing hand. "Where was your brother this morning? He was supposed to help me raise the walls."

"Actually, I came to find you on Everett's behalf." Her smile faded. "Another lamb went missing last night and Everett left the house before breakfast this morning. He searched until dark when a lamb disappeared three days ago, and I assumed he would do the same today. I knew you expected him to help with your house, so I came to tell you."

Levi regretted his accusatory tone. He looked across the wide green pasture to his left. The Fosters' land stretched to the west as far as the horizon. "Your father has a couple hundred sheep. Why is Everett so concerned with a lamb or two?"

"The lambs are precious to Everett. He names them and knows every one of them as if they were his children." She shook her head. "The disappearance of two lambs in less than a week is troubling. He and my father are both quite mystified."

Though he heard her full and smooth voice, he was too engrossed in his injured hand to respond. He held up his arm, and a stream of blood dripped from his elbow. He would get the stitches, but he wouldn't suspend the work on his house.

Mandy continued her chatter as they walked across the Colburn property to Lydia's medical cottage. Levi hoped his father wouldn't be outside and was relieved to make it past the main house and to the cottage without being noticed.

Mandy didn't bother knocking on the cottage door. She opened it and immediately sang out, "Doctor Bradshaw, you have a patient." Levi rolled his eyes.

Lydia wasn't inside the entry-level medical office. Levi walked to the staircase and looked up to the door of Lydia and Connor's bedroom. Though his sister had been married for over a year, he still couldn't take the thought of her upstairs alone with her husband. He considered sending Mandy up to get Lydia when the door opened.

Lydia descended the stairs. "Good Morning, Levi." She smiled at him, but then shock replaced her gracious welcome as her eyes landed on his bloody hand. "What have you done?" She hurried him to the patient cot then unwrapped the ruined shirt from his hand and examined the damage. She turned to the cabinets on the wall near the cot. He caught her rapid movements in his peripheral vision, but he didn't look at her. Medicine bottles clanked, followed by the sound of liquid pouring.

Lydia returned to the cot with a shallow pan half-filled with tepid water. She washed his wound and wiped it with a rag dipped in oil from the gray leaf tree. The oil's pungent fumes made him blink. Lydia grinned. "It's strong, I know. This is a new method I have developed. The gray leaf penetrates the injury more rapidly."

"Are you going to experiment on me while I bleed to—" His question dissipated as the power of the gray leaf tree seeped into his hand and engaged his system. His nerves settled and heat flowed into his body where the blood had drained out. His breath steadied and euphoric warmth slowed his pulse. Something tingled deep in his hand as the gray leaf's strength overpowered his pain. Then the sensation was gone and so was the pain.

He gazed up at Mandy, who stood near the cot pulling a curl of hair through her fingers. With the gray leaf medicine coursing through his veins, his heart didn't ache when he looked at her. Her fingertips swirled the cord of red hair around and around until the curl was as taut as a spring. Her mouth moved as she spoke to Lydia with that fluid voice. He liked the sound of it until he realized Mandy was talking about him.

"He nearly ripped his hand off trying to raise his house by himself. He didn't want to come to you at all, but I forced him. I'm not sure what he would have done if I hadn't arrived when I did. He bled the entire mile walk here."

"I can speak for myself, Amanda." Levi straightened his posture in an effort to retain some of his dignity. He felt childish sitting there on the patient cot with two women fussing over him, though the humiliation was a faint echo of what it would be if his father walked in. The relief brought by the gray leaf had also given him a slight sense of apathy, which he found unusual and comforting.

Lydia prepared a suture, then she sat on the cot beside him. She pulled his hand onto her lap and began stitching to close the wound. He looked away and noticed Mandy's face as she watched the needle. Her fingers halted their curl twirling and her nostrils flared. Though her queasiness gave him a twinge of satisfaction, he wanted her to leave. "Thank you for your valiant effort in seeing me to the doctor, Mandy. You're free to go now."

Mandy turned her back to them and faced the window for a moment. "Yes, perhaps I will be going." She had her hand over her stomach, and he almost felt pity for her.

"Thank you for helping my brother, Mandy." Lydia's eyes focused on her stitching. She didn't look up as Mandy left the cottage.

Levi stared at his hand, surprised that watching the needle and thread pass in and out of his flesh didn't bother him. The numbness from the gray leaf oil made his arm feel as if it were detached from his body. He doubted he would ever understand the wonders of medicine as Lydia did, but he was grateful nonetheless.

Lydia tied a knot and cut the silk thread. "I assume Mandy spoke the truth—you did this working alone." He gave no reply. Lydia glanced at him before she stood and stepped over to the countertop next to the patient cot. "The village needs your carpentry skills, but you won't be able to work if you get your hands ripped off. And you are a grown man, so I shouldn't scold you."

"Father will do it for you."

"No, I don't think he will." She took a small jar of gray leaf salve from the cabinet and returned to the cot. Then she covered his stitched palm with a thick layer of the ointment and began to wrap his hand in a clean gauzy bandage. "Father has granted you the freedom you desired and the land to build your own house. Perhaps he took longer to come to that decision than your patience afforded. Regardless, he has yet to present the hostility you seem to expect from him."

From where he sat on the patient cot, Levi could see out the front window of Lydia's office. Between the thin curtains he had a clear view of the back door to the home he was born in. The imposing structure cast a shadow over her cottage, just as it had over his life. "Things may have changed some because of Connor's arrival, but I don't feel this great sense of acceptance from Father like you do."

Lydia finished bandaging his hand and he examined it. The gray leaf medicine kept it numb. "Thank you."

"You're welcome." She piled the bloody rags in a ceramic bowl and lifted a corner of his once-beige shirt, which was now drenched in red. "I believe this is ruined." She released the garment and wiped her hands, then pointed at his arm. "Move your fingers."

He wiggled his fingertips under the gauzy material to demonstrate their dexterity. "Much better." He stood to leave, believing the ordeal was over.

"You haven't been released from my care." She lifted an eyebrow and smiled as she stepped to her desk. "Lie back for a few minutes. I'll tell you when you can go, but you won't be returning to work today. Your injury will heal quickly and completely, but you must rest."

The medicine left him lightheaded—or perhaps it was the loss of blood—but he would never confess it. He sighed and obeyed the doctor, even though she was his sister. Stretching his legs out on the cot, he laid his bandaged hand across his bare chest. No matter how he tried to center his thoughts on his building plans—even the pleasure of being sated by the smell of freshly hewn lumber—his mind continually returned to the fantasy of one day sharing his house with Mandy.

Someone tapped on the cottage door, filling him with the dread of being seen injured by his father. The door opened a crack, but he couldn't see who it was from his position on the patient cot. It frustrated him because he was the one who hinged the door in that direction when he helped his father build the cottage for Lydia. Of course when he hung the door, he never imagined someday he would be the patient on the cot with the obscured view. Then he heard Bethany's voice.

Lydia stayed seated at her desk and motioned with the pen in her hand as she spoke to their youngest sister. "I have a patient at the moment, Bethany. What do you need?"

Though grateful for Lydia's discretion, Levi decided it would be better to let Bethany see him and know he was fine than let her hear about his injury later and worry about him. He propped himself up on his elbows. "I'm fine, Lydia. Let her come in."

"Levi?" Bethany craned her head around the door. As soon as her eyes landed on his bandaged arm she gasped and covered her mouth with her hand. She rushed to the patient cot and knelt on the wood floor. "Oh, Levi! What happened to you? Are you all right?"

"I just needed a couple stitches. I'm fine, Beth."

"Where is your shirt?"

He pointed to the pile of blood-drenched rags on the countertop. Bethany looked at it then squealed and fanned herself with frantic motions. "Oh, Levi!"

He chuckled at her dramatic gestures. "I'm fine, really. Lydia stitched me up. It turns out she can sew more than curtains."

Lydia chortled and continued writing at her desk.

Bethany wrinkled her nose. "How did this happen?"

"It was nothing, really." Levi lay back on the cot and studied Bethany. She wore a dress she usually reserved for Sundays, and her hair was down except for a section on one side that was pinned back to reveal her ear. She put her hand on his arm, and he noticed the silver charm bracelet at her wrist. "You aren't dressed for working at the pottery yard. Where are you off to today?"

Bethany's face relaxed and she smiled at him. "Mrs. Vestal is firing the kiln, so she gave me the day off. I'm going to Phoebe's. Her mother is making pastries and we are taking some when we call on Mrs. Ashton. Then we're going to visit the Owenses in the afternoon." Her sincere smile reached her eyes and kept the blue sparkling while she looked at him, but her smile vanished and her brow furrowed each time she glanced at his bandaged hand. She freely exposed her emotions, probably because she never had cause to conceal them.

"You'll make Mrs. Ashton and the Owenses happy." He patted the top of her hand. "You should get going."

"Will you be all right? I can stay if you need me."

He smiled at his sweet sister—not yet seventeen and worried over him. "I'm fine, Beth, really."

She stood and held up a finger. "Oh, and Mrs. Vestal asked if you could build another set of shelves in the shed at the pottery yard. She says she needs more storage space because I produce more pieces in a week than any of her past apprentices made in a month."

"He won't be building any shelves today," Lydia chimed from her desk.

Levi glanced at Lydia then looked up at Bethany. "I have already spoken with Mrs. Vestal. She knows I will resume work around the village after I have finished the house."

"And he isn't working on that today either," Lydia added.

Bethany made a face at their sister's comment, but Lydia didn't look up from her notes in time to see it. Levi winked at Bethany. She bent and kissed his cheek then marched to the door.

* * *

Though Mandy spent the morning taking Levi to get stitches, her creative energy returned as soon as she got back to her workshop, and it remained strong throughout the day. As the light outside her window faded, she set her chisel on the workbench and used both hands to wrap her auburn curls in a tight swirl behind her head. She jabbed a piece of sharpened dowel rod through the middle of the bun to hold her hair in place, but she knew the rebellious curls would defect one sweaty spring at a time. Returning her attention to her work, she gently blew away the fine wood shavings sprinkled across what was now the scroll of a violin. She lifted an unfinished instrument body from the shelf above her workbench and tapped lightly in several places, checking the tone and clarity of the gray leaf wood. Pleased with the balance of the pure rich sound, she dipped a thin brush into a well of animal glue and began the process of binding the saddle to the sun-dried body of the violin. After clamping the glued pieces together to dry overnight, she removed her apron and shook the wood dust from the sleeves of her dress.

Entranced by hours alone in her workshop in the loft of her family's barn, she jumped when her father appeared in the doorway. She covered her heart with her hand. "You startled me."

"Sorry, love. I didn't mean to." Samuel Foster's ruddy cheeks rounded as he spoke. "I'm hunting for my pliers. Have you seen them?"

She shook her head as she draped her apron over a peg on the wall near her workbench and then motioned to the cluttered shelves by the door. "They're probably in that mess."

While he rifled through the shelves of heaped tools, she stepped to the open window and fanned the cool evening air into the collar of her dress. She looked down across the expansive green pasture that stretched to the fading horizon. As the last light of the summer sun disappeared for the day, a lonely ache began to set in. Thinking of her brother's search for the lost lambs, she turned to her father. "Did Everett find his sheep?"

Samuel was balancing on his tiptoes as he inspected an upper shelf. He didn't respond, so she tried again. "Father?"

"Hm?" He stopped shuffling tools and exhaled, causing his cheeks to puff under his pure white beard. "Everett? Oh, the poor lad searched all day. He's quite torn up over the missing lambs. Rightly so—it's terribly peculiar. Fifty-six years on this farm and I've yet to lose a sheep. He has lost two in less than a week."

She too felt sorry for her brother—though Everett was no longer a *lad*. "Is he still out searching?" She walked to the messy shelf, reached straight for the pliers, and held them out to Samuel. When he lowered from his tiptoes they stood eye to eye.

"No, I sent him inside for the night. Your mother is getting dinner ready." He took the pliers and patted them on the thick palm of his hand. Then he pointed at the unfinished instrument on Mandy's workbench. "Are you still working, or will you be joining us for dinner this evening?"

She glanced at the violin she had spent the day carving. She wanted to keep working late into the night while her energy was high, but felt she should go to Everett. She stepped away from the workbench. "I'll be right in."

He nodded, and she expected him to leave. Instead, he raised his wooly eyebrows and stepped farther into the spacious workshop. "I haven't been up here in a while. My knees aren't fond of climbing the steps to the loft." He rubbed the bald spot on top of his head and smiled at her. "When you were little, you would sit up here for hours watching your grandfather. He must have repaired your old violin a dozen times before the two of you decided to try to build a new one. He would be proud to know that you have made a profession out of his hobby." He walked over to a recently completed violin and chuckled as he ran a finger over the varnished inlay. "Can you imagine what he would think if he heard one of your instruments made of the gray leaf wood?"

She smiled and pulled the dowel rod out of her hair, sending curls down her back. "I think about that often while I work. Grandfather's willow and maple violins were fine instruments, but there is no sound comparable to gray leaf wood."

"So true, so true." He grinned as he spoke. Moving away from the row of unfinished instruments, he thumped the pliers against his thigh. He stepped to the door, then he turned back and opened his mouth as if he wanted to say something. But he only closed it again and nodded as he glanced around the workshop.

She nodded too. "Please, tell Mother I will be right there."

"Very well," he said as he walked out the door.

Before Mandy left her workshop, she tossed the dowel onto her bench and took one last look out the window. The sky was a deep shade of lavender with a few wisps of shadowy black cloud. The summertime dusk stoked the song of crickets and an unsettling discontent she tried her best to ignore. The only certain—yet temporary—antidote for her recurring evening doldrums came in the form of *intrigue*, but the farther she advanced from the age where flirtation was considered acceptable in the village, the more her chances of a cure waned.

She looked away from the darkening sky and sighed. She tried not to focus on the old and frequent feeling, but the company of her loving family was a sure exacerbation. When intrigue wasn't possible, the only way to get through that first bleak hour after dusk was to go for a walk alone. The settling darkness and the freedom of being alone on the road always soothed her spirit. She longed to walk the road into the village, but tonight Everett needed her, so solitude wasn't an option. She propped the workshop door open to allow the evening air to circulate throughout the loft, and as she walked away, she glanced back into the darkening room. The hollow feeling inside her chest grew, causing her to wonder what purpose such emptiness could serve.

As she walked through the loft, she looked over the railing to the expansive barn floor below. With the flock out to pasture for the summer, the barn was quiet save for the occasional sound of the horses in their stalls on the other end of the massive building. The barn's wide doors had been rolled closed for the day, so she descended the steps and walked out the side door toward the house.

The air was warm, but it felt good to be outdoors after a long day in her workshop. The oval moon was beginning to spill its bluish light on the yard and the vegetable garden and the back porch of her family's home. Everett was standing on the porch with his hands planted on the railing and his head down. Mandy climbed the steps and stood beside him. She waited for a moment, then she leaned her hands on the railing also. "I'm sorry about your lambs."

Everett turned his head a degree and glanced at her before looking off into the distance. He gave no vocal response, nor did she expect him to. She stared at the black blur of nighttime horizon. "Are the dogs with the flock?"

"Of course."

She glanced back at the oldest of their four herding dogs lying on the mat by the back door. "Except Shep. He's lucky if he can make it from the front porch to the back anymore." She looked at Everett, but he didn't acknowledge her remark. She dropped her gaze to the railing and traced the wood grain in the gray leaf board with her fingertip. "Do you think some kind of animal took the lambs?"

"Like what?"

"I don't know... a bear or a lion?" She grinned. "Like the ones David fought in the Bible."

"We don't have predatory animals in the Land."

Roseanna Foster tapped on the glass of the back door. Mandy glanced over her shoulder at her mother and raised a finger. Roseanna nodded and stepped away from the window.

Mandy looked back at Everett. "Levi tried to raise the wall frames by himself this morning."

"Tried? Wasn't he successful?"

She shook her head. "Only with the first two frames. A rope nearly ripped his hand off when he tried to raise the third wall. I had to take him to Lydia for stitches."

"I forgot all about helping him." Everett looked at her, and his brow creased in the center. "Was he angry with me?"

"When I went to tell him you weren't coming, I found him writhing in pain and angry with himself on top of his usual petulance, so who can tell?"

Everett returned his gaze to the western pastures. "That's not a very respectful attitude."

"You're right. I should show him some pity, shouldn't I?"

"No. He doesn't want your pity."

"Oh, I know what he wants from me," she laughed.

"No." Everett pushed away from the railing and stepped to the door. "He wants your respect."

She had never considered respecting Levi. He was her best friend's brother and one of the many men who had once been intrigued with her—a combination that hardly warranted respect in her estimation. She didn't agree with Everett, but after a moment's rumination, she said, "I know he does."

Mandy gave Shep a pat on the head as she walked across the porch. Everett held the door open for her and she stepped into the kitchen to spend the evening having dinner with her family, wishing she had stayed in her workshop.

CHAPTER TWO

L evi piled fresh hay into the feeders in each barn stall and hoped he could make the chore last until dinnertime. He stopped and leaned the pitchfork against the splintered wall, then he stretched the palm of his hand wide to relieve the lingering stiffness from his injury. As he reached for the pitchfork, Connor stepped into the barn and motioned to the feeders. "I was on my way to do that, but I guess you beat me to it."

Levi looked at Connor's dress clothes and raised an eyebrow. "Tell the truth: Lydia and Bethany ran you out of the kitchen. When will you learn to stay away from that room when the women are preparing for a party?"

Connor grinned and shrugged. "I asked Lydia if I could help with anything and she sent me to the barn."

"Wait until Adeline and Maggie get here. Then even my father will be wandering around the yard looking for chores."

"That bad, huh?" Connor grimaced. "I told Lydia not to go to all this trouble for me, but she said I'll only turn thirty once."

"She finds a reason to summon our eldest sisters here from Woodland every few months." Levi walked out of the barn but left the doors open. "As long as I'm not the reason for the attention, it's fine with me. It gives me a chance to see my niece and nephews."

Connor walked beside him toward the house. "Hopefully, you'll have another niece or nephew soon... I mean... nothing yet, but we are sure trying."

Levi groaned at the thought. "I know Lydia is your wife, but she is also my sister. So I'd rather you keep your efforts to yourself."

Connor laughed then glanced at the road when a wagon turned onto the property. Levi lifted a hand and waved as the wagon approached. His brother-in-law drove and Maggie sat on the bench seat with her two-year-old son on her lap. She struggled to subdue little Seth's excited bounces as the wagon rattled to a stop.

Levi met the wagon beside the house and reached for his youngest nephew. A piercing squeal of laughter escaped Seth's throat and echoed off the house as Levi swung the toddler overhead in a playful circle. Maggie greeted him then fussed over Seth's rumpled clothing. After accepting a slobbery kiss from the giddy toddler, he returned Seth to his anxious mother.

An open carriage drove onto the property. Though Levi didn't recognize the unusual carriage, he watched as his eldest sister, Adeline, her husband and two young children smiled and waved. When the carriage stopped behind Maggie's wagon, Levi opened its door and his niece and nephew vaulted to the ground.

"Uncle Levi! Uncle Levi!" The two children furled their arms around him while they simultaneously blared rapid, unrelated tales, competing to capture his attention.

"Gabe! Hannah!" he beamed.

Flanked by the children, he offered his hand to his sister. Adeline took it and stepped down from the carriage. "I waited until yesterday morning to tell the children we were coming here. They prattled nonstop about their Uncle Levi the entire journey." She halted in front of Levi and put her hands on either side of his face. "I may never get used to seeing my little brother all grown up."

Adeline resembled their mother to such a striking degree it pained him to look her in the eye for long. He kissed Adeline's cheek. "It's good to see you, Addie."

As Adeline walked to the house, Levi tapped his knuckles on the carriage and turned to his brother-in-law. "Did you build this?"

The man nodded and began to relate the process to Levi. It interested him; however, the two young children pulling at his arms interfered with his concentration. He reached down and tickled the children, then he pretended to snarl, setting off the chase through the yard that he intended. He caught the giggling children and carried one under each arm, but when he noticed his father at the carriage, he stopped walking. He wanted to go inspect the carriage and learn about its construction, but not with his father there. He set the children down and glanced at the carriage, wishing he could forgive his father and enjoy his company like everyone else. Instead, he bent and picked a tiny yellow daisy from the grass and offered it to his niece. She giggled as she accepted the flower.

Adeline popped her head out of the back door and called them into the house. Little Hannah ran to her mother and Gabe jumped onto Levi's back, pretending his uncle was a horse. Levi obliged and galloped to the house. Before he reached the kitchen, the aroma of the food wafted out the door, causing his stomach to respond with a growl.

Lydia handed a stack of plates to Adeline and glanced at Levi as he walked into the kitchen. A strand of hair dropped across her forehead and dangled between her eyes. "Levi, would you please get Aunt Isabella? We're almost ready to eat."

"Sure." He deposited his nephew in front of Connor. "Gabe, wish your Uncle Connor a happy birthday then show him your loose tooth."

Levi scanned the feast that was being arranged on the buffet, then he hurried through the parlor and down the hallway to his great-aunt's room. The farther he moved from the kitchen, the more muffled the happy sound of the family's overlapping conversations became. Isabella's door was closed. He knocked but couldn't hear whether or not she had responded, so he turned the glass knob and opened the door a crack. "Aunt Isabella?"

"Come in, Levi." Her raspy voice came between audible breaths. "Close the door behind you, please."

He obeyed but regretted Isabella's request as it silenced the sound of the family gathering. Her room was dim and stuffy. She was sitting on the edge of her unmade bed. He spoke as he stepped closer to her so she would know he was approaching. "Dinner is ready. The girls really outdid themselves with the food. Are you ready to join us?"

"Fetch my cane, would you?" She waved her hand in the direction of the chair where she usually sat to do her knitting, but he noticed the cane was propped against the bedside table.

He touched it to her hand. "Here it is."

She grabbed the cane's handle and drew it close to her body. "Oh, yes. I must have forgotten where I left it. Is it dinnertime already?"

"Yes." He knelt in front of his elderly aunt. "Are you feeling well?"

"Of course, child. My afternoon nap just went a little long today." Her eyes roamed as she spoke. "Has everyone arrived?"

"Yes. Adeline and Maggie are here with their families. They are eager to see you."

She nodded. "It does my heart good to have everyone together. And for such a joyous occasion, too—Isaac's birthday."

"It's Connor's birthday."

"Of course, Connor's birthday. That's what I said." Isabella's lips continued to move after she spoke, and Levi knew she had more to say. He put his hand on hers and waited. She cleared her throat, but her voice remained raspy. "After your mother passed, I prayed God would allow me to live long enough to see all five of you children find your place in the world. I worry about you so. I just want to know each of you will be loved when I'm gone." She smiled then. "Adeline and Maggie didn't waste time on the matter—both married and already have children—and now Lydia has Connor. Bethany's beautiful spirit will no doubt collect her many suitors as soon as your father lets her court. However, you… well, I suppose boys are different. It bothers me—your being alone."

"Aunt Isabella, I—"

"You are building that house alone." She patted his hand. "And look what that got you—not two days ago you tore your hand open. It was only by the grace of God you didn't rip it off completely. No salve will reattach a hand, child, I assure you."

He nodded before he realized she wouldn't see his gesture. "Please, don't worry. I was just unprepared to raise the walls by myself. Lydia has already forced me to promise I will be more careful. And Connor is going to help me build while school is out."

"And once the house is built, you will live there alone." She raised a finger before he could reply. "That's your choice and I don't wish to inflict guilt, but it's time you sought a wife. Perhaps no young ladies are available in Good Springs. There are seven other villages in the Land. Go, Levi. Search for a wife. It's not good for a man to be alone."

He chuckled and stood. "Before I do, may I eat dinner?"

Isabella laughed and held his arm. She steadied her cane in front of her and took slow steps toward the door. "Of course, you could save yourself all the trouble of traveling and simply try again for Miss Foster's affection."

"Thank you, Aunt Isabella." He forced a smile as he spoke and refrained from letting out the heavy sigh that weighed upon his chest, knowing his aunt drew conclusions from the slightest perceptible clue. With each step they inched closer to the door. Relief washed over him when he opened the door and the sounds of the family celebration flowed from the kitchen.

Levi escorted Isabella to her usual seat at the nearest end of the long kitchen table. Lydia had filled a plate for Isabella at the buffet, and she set it in front of their aunt. Levi sat with Isabella until the rest of family came to the table with their plates. Only then did he go to the buffet and fill his plate. He returned to the table and took his seat next to his father with his back to the hearth. With extra chairs squeezed in on the table's long sides, and his brother-in-law and Gabe sitting nearby on the seat-level stone hearth, Levi was amazed the whole family fit in the kitchen.

Before they ate, John Colburn said a prayer; his tone was the same blend of authority and humility he used during his weekly church sermons. The tone evidenced John's belief in his status over the people and under God. After the prayer, forks clinked and compliments flowed to the cooks.

Levi glanced from one face to the next as he ate. The new blend of the growing family left few similarities in features. Adeline resembled their mother. Lydia shared his coloring—light brown hair and light brown eyes. People always told Levi he had his father's build and mannerisms, though even the slightest comparison to his father rankled. He looked over his shoulder at his nephew seated on the hearth and thought Gabe resembled a Colburn, though the boy's father was a McIntosh.

John tapped his spoon against his glass, commanding the party's attention. "We gather today to celebrate Connor's birthday." He looked at Connor. "Though today you celebrate thirty years of life on earth, it is the last two years of your life in the Land that are my cause for celebration. Your providential arrival here saved you from the misery of a world at war. It also blessed me with your friendship, blessed my daughter with your love, and blessed our village with your knowledge. I thank God you were brought into my family. May He bless you all of your days. Happy birthday, Connor!"

* * *

Mandy shielded her eyes from the morning sun as she walked past the Colburn property. Gravel pebbles crackled under her heels with each step. She stopped on the road and smiled when she spotted Lydia stepping out of her cottage door.

Lydia waved. "Are you going to the market?"

"I'm on my way now." Mandy raised her voice to carry across the yard. "Do you need me to get anything for you?"

Lydia lifted the front of her skirt and hurried to the road. "Maybe a trader has brought my order of glass from Stonehill. Do you mind if I join you?"

"Please do." Mandy resumed her walk to the village once Lydia came beside her. The breeze blew a salty scent in from the nearby shore. A wagon rattled down the road behind them, so they stepped into the grass along the side of the road and waited for it to pass. Mandy didn't recognize the man driving the wagon, but he winked at her as he passed. She responded with a playful smile, and then looked at the village ahead. She loved the Saturday market in Good Springs and felt excited as she watched the crowds gather in the distance.

The morning sun lit the steeple and the front of the white chapel as they walked through the shadow of the stone library. Many of the village's farmers, craftsmen, and artists were at their booths in the sandy lot beside the library. Mandy raised her heels for a better view as she scanned the market hoping to see a particular traveling trader among the vendors.

"What are you looking for?" Lydia asked as she too gazed about the crowd.

"I need strings." Mandy lowered her heels. "I was hoping the trader from Riverside came today; he sometimes has catgut."

"I despise that word." Lydia gave a small shiver. "Come. I think I see the trader over there." Lydia tugged at Mandy's sleeve and guided her through the crowd.

As Mandy approached the trader's booth, he held a finger up to the man speaking to him. Both men smiled at her, and she felt a jolt of satisfaction from their obvious delight in her appearance. Noticing the trader's strong jaw and broad shoulders, she made sure her posture presented her figure well. The trader and his customer both eyed her with desire, boosting her enjoyment in the nonverbal exchange.

The trader tilted his whiskered chin toward her. "Ah, it's the Land's best luthier. Have you come to make a trade?"

"I have." Mandy smiled and leaned toward the trader, then she heard Lydia click her tongue. She ignored Lydia's sound of disapproval and pulled a curl through her fingers. She gave it a slow twirl. "I need strings. Have you any catgut today?"

"I have." The trader grinned, revealing a row of rotten teeth. He bent and rifled through a crate on the ground then stood holding a wound heap of the particular type of string she needed.

Disappointed in the flaw she found in the man's appearance, Mandy dropped her curl and stepped back beside Lydia. She glanced at the string then at the trader. Her voice omitted its usual sultry inflection. "What do you require in trade?"

"Have you any new instruments available? Your work is requested in every village."

Mandy knew her instruments claimed more in trade than the strings she placed on them. She glanced at Lydia then looked back at the trader. "Do you have the doctor's order of glass?"

The trader shifted his gaze to Lydia. "Three crates from Stonehill?"

Lydia nodded. "Yes. Medicine jars."

"I have them," he confirmed.

Mandy moved forward. "One violin for the catgut *and* the order of glass."

"I accept." He grinned again, causing Mandy to blink and look away. He looked at Lydia. "Are you the wife of Connor Bradshaw?"

"I am," Lydia replied.

The trader stooped to a crate on the other side of his booth and produced a burlap-wrapped package about the size of a dinner plate. He handed it to Lydia. "This was sent to your husband by the overseer of Stonehill. He said it is private and of utmost importance." She accepted the package and hugged it to her chest while Mandy finalized the arrangements with the trader.

When Mandy and Lydia walked away, Mandy glanced at the package. "What do you think it is?"

"I don't know."

"You are holding it as if it's precious."

The edge of Lydia's mouth curved up. "I am simply delighted to be a wife entrusted with an important package."

"And private. Don't forget that detail." Mandy grinned and reached a finger to the cord tied around the package. "Let's have a look."

"Stop it." Lydia laughed and pulled away. "Connor is at the chapel with my father. Surely you can behave yourself long enough to deliver a package."

Mandy followed her through the crowd at the market, across the cobblestone street to the church, and up the chapel steps. The church's tall doors were propped open with wooden wedges, and the women stepped inside. The dim sanctuary smelled like candlewax and old books. When Mandy's eyes adjusted to the change in light, she saw Connor walking out of John's office at the opposite end of the long, empty chapel. She watched his face as he spotted Lydia. He lowered his chin and grinned as he moved toward his wife. When he reached Lydia, he drew her into a kiss. Mandy tried to be polite and look away; still, her lips pressed together in response to the affectionate display. She began to imagine what it would feel like to kiss a man she truly loved, but knowing she could never allow herself to love like that, she stopped the fantasy at once.

Lydia gave Connor the package and relayed the trader's message about its importance. His brow creased as he unfolded a small note attached to the package. Mandy's curiosity stirred. She stepped closer. "Perhaps it's a late birthday present."

"Nope." He leaned his shoulder into the wall and crossed his legs at the ankle as he read the note. Then he looked at Lydia. "It's from Wade Vestal, the overseer of Stonehill. He says this object was found in a creek bed near their village."

Mandy watched as Connor untied the cord around the package and drew a strange piece of black matter from the burlap. He held the object in one hand and looked at it, then he flipped it over and studied the other side. The edges of the object looked as if it had been through fire.

"What is it?" Lydia and Mandy asked at the same time, then glanced at each other and giggled.

Connor shrugged. "It's a piece of plastic."

Lydia touched the black object. "We don't have plastic in the Land."

"That's probably why Wade sent it to me." He glanced at Lydia. "I think it is debris from the jet crash."

Lydia raised her eyebrows. "Your airplane exploded over the ocean near Good Springs—

Stonehill is one hundred eighty miles away from here. And that was nearly two years ago."

Connor drew a breath. "A couple of hundred miles is nothing in terms of a debris field. And Wade said it was found in a creek bed, so it could have been carried there by the water."

Lydia bit her bottom lip. "What do you think it means for the Land? Will we be discovered by the outside world? Will we be invaded?"

He tucked the piece of plastic back into the burlap then wrapped one arm around Lydia. "Please don't worry about this, okay?"

Lydia looked up at him. "But you always say we should hope the Land remains undetectable to the outside world because of the war."

He kissed the top of Lydia's head and kept his arm around her. "Let me handle it, okay?" His low voice held an intimate quality that made Mandy both happy for Lydia and jealous of her.

Mandy looked away and hoped another man like Connor would somehow, someday come to the Land. She grinned and looked back at Lydia. "Perhaps another airplane has crashed sending another eligible warrior into the Land?"

Connor and Lydia looked at each other then chuckled at her.

She batted her eyelashes and tilted her head. "Well... one can only hope."

CHAPTER THREE

The warm kitchen of the Colburn home smelled like fresh bread and baked chicken long after the table was cleared from the evening meal. Propped open, the back door allowed night air to cool the room. Two oil lamps—one at each end of the long kitchen table—provided the only light as Levi rhythmically dropped playing cards in small piles. "Full deck with a draw."

Mandy sat across the table from him and looked at the cards that landed in front of her. "Must we play by Connor's rules? There are four of us—we could play bluff by the old rules."

"Personally, I don't care." Connor grinned as he sat in the chair beside Levi. "I will win either way."

Isabella snickered in the other room. She only stayed up late when there was a chance to live vicariously through young people. Lydia sat beside Mandy and smiled, but Mandy only put her chin on her fist and scowled. "Having a draw takes the game from one of chance to one of skill. I prefer bluff. A game is more fun when it's just chance."

Levi finished dealing the cards. Each player picked up the hand dealt and examined the cards privately. Levi rearranged the order of his cards and glanced at Mandy. "But you actually get to bluff when there is a draw."

"Yes, and that requires skill," Connor added.

"That depends on the opponent..." Levi leaned back in his chair and gazed at Mandy. She was beautiful in the lamplight. She was beautiful in any light, but thinking about her beauty only dimmed his spirit. "It requires skill to discern a man's bluff. Attempting to gauge a woman's bluff doesn't require skill—it requires clairvoyance."

Connor laughed. Mandy briefly feigned offense, then her pink lips curved into a smile. Lydia laughed, too, then she looked at Connor and they started to nuzzle. They wouldn't want to play cards for very long.

Levi groaned and checked his cards—three kings, an ace, and a six. He moved only his eyes as he studied the other players. Connor sighed but otherwise maintained a stoic expression. Mandy's face was unreadable. She liked to pretend to be incapable of pretending, but he wasn't fooled.

Lydia smiled at her cards and asked, "Does a four-of-a-kind beat a flush even if the cards are low numbers?"

"Lydia." Connor dragged out her name in mock disappointment and drew his brows together.

"Oh, sorry." Lydia bit her lip after she apologized. "It's been a long time since I played this game."

Mandy slid three cards to Levi. He took them and dealt her three new cards. He could feel her watching his face and decided to forgo making eye contact. He looked at Lydia. "How many?"

"Just one, thank you." Lydia grinned. Connor shook his head at her and then laid three cards on the table. Levi took Connor's discards and dealt three more.

"One for the dealer." Levi examined his new hand—four kings and an ace. A favorable hand occurred with such infrequence that it required considerable focus to suppress his astonishment. He controlled his expression and looked at Mandy for her play.

She blew out a heavy breath and laid her cards face down on the table. "I fold."

"I'm in for three." Lydia reached to the small bowl of wooden marbles in front of her, took three, and set them near a larger bowl in the center of the table.

Levi picked them up and dropped them into the large bowl. "Connor?"

"I'll call." Connor added three marbles to the bowl, one at a time.

Levi tried to conceal his confidence as he set three of his pieces into the bowl. He looked at Mandy—though she was out of the round, it was natural for his eyes to move to her. She leaned back and scanned Lydia's cards. Her eyes grew wide.

Levi waited for his sister's move. "Lydia?" She shook her head.

He looked at Connor. Connor glanced at Lydia and then at Levi and raised one eyebrow. His countenance reminded Levi of the first few weeks after Connor's arrival in the Land. Levi had been suspicious of the strange warrior then and—though it was in a friendly, competitive way now—he was equally suspicious. Connor slid three more marbles to the center of the table. "I'll raise."

Levi matched then looked at Lydia. She was looking at Mandy as if expecting advice. Mandy shrugged and Lydia tossed her cards onto the table. "I'm out."

Levi and Connor sat glaring at each other with their cards concealed. Mandy and Lydia both giggled. Levi moved first. "Let's see them, brother." Connor spread his cards on the table, revealing a flush of diamonds. Levi grinned and displayed his four kings. Connor laughed and shook his hand. The women laughed. While Connor took the large bowl and poured its contents into Levi's bowl, Lydia picked up her empty water glass and walked to the sink. Mandy got up and followed Lydia. The two women stood near the sink whispering. Levi collected the cards, shuffled the deck twice, and set it in front of Mandy's chair. Then he glanced over his shoulder at her.

Connor nudged him. "Why don't you do something about that?"

"About what?" He kept his voice down.

"Obviously, you're in love with Mandy. Why don't you ask her out?"

"I tried to court her once. She rejected me."

"Yeah, when you were both, what, seventeen?" Connor lifted a palm. "That was six years ago. You're a man now. I think you have a chance."

"If I have learned one thing about Mandy Foster in the past six years, it's that no man has a chance." He started to push his hands through his hair then stopped and turned when he heard Everett Foster's voice at the door.

Lydia welcomed Everett inside. Mandy took her brother's arm and led him to the table. "Come, join our game." Her voice sang in excitement as she picked up the card deck and sat in her chair. "We've only played one round—Levi won. I'm sure you won't mind if Everett joins us, will you, Levi?"

Everett remained standing and put his hand over the cards. "Actually, I didn't come here to play cards. There is something I need to discuss with Levi and Connor." His young face was wrinkled with worry. Mandy and Lydia glanced at each other and left the room. They went into the parlor and started talking with Isabella.

"What is it?" Connor asked Everett as soon as the men were alone.

Everett lowered his voice. "Where is Bethany?"

"She's at a friend's house tonight," Levi answered. "What's wrong?"

Everett glanced at the open doorway that led from the kitchen to the parlor, then he leaned toward Levi and Connor. "Last week I had two lambs go missing. I had all but given up my search, and then today I decided to ride out to the western portion of our property. I went to the creek near the boulder outcrops and found a campsite."

Levi glanced at Connor, who lifted both hands gesturing his need for more information. So Levi looked back at Everett. "Possibly your father's farmhands?"

"No. We only had two men help with the shearing this year, and they moved on to Southpoint weeks ago." Everett's dark hair dropped onto his forehead and he gave his head a quick jerk to send it back. "It looked to me as if someone had camped there for a while. There were wheel marks in the dirt, probably from a wagon. I could tell they had horses and... I found the bones of the lambs."

Connor's brow furrowed. "I've only been in the Land a couple of years, but most people here seem to live by a fairly strict code of ethics. This sounds like vagrant behavior." He looked at Levi. "Do you know anyone in Good Springs who would steal a lamb for dinner?"

Levi shook his head. He felt sorry for Everett but was more concerned for the safety of the Fosters and the village. He could still hear the women chatting in the parlor. He looked at Connor and whispered, "It could be Felix and his sons."

Connor nodded. "Maybe they have come to return your wagon."

Everett's eyes bounced from Levi to Connor and back. "Felix and his sons? The men you fought outside of Northcrest when you were traveling?"

"Yes," Levi answered. He thought of the robbery during his journey with Connor—and the home invasion a decade prior that caused the death of his mother. "Everett, what did your father say when you told him about the campsite?"

"He said to tell you and Connor—and your father, if he is here."

Levi shook his head. "Father is counseling a family in the village this evening."

Everett pointed to the parlor. "He also said not to tell the women."

"Of course—no need to frighten them," Levi agreed. Then he looked to Connor. "Do you think it could be someone from the outside world?"

Connor picked up his water glass and made the liquid inside it swirl; he stared at the glass and clenched his jaw. "If someone from the war came into the Land, I doubt they would drive a wagon and roast lamb over a campfire. The way the world is right now, if the Unified States or any other military force invaded the Land, there wouldn't be a lamb left... or a drop of clean water for that matter. In my two years here I have only heard of one group of outlaws in this land—Felix and his two sons."

Everett's gaze continued to shift between Levi and Connor. Though Everett wasn't yet nineteen, Levi had noticed his growth in strength and maturity. "Everett, you have been sparring with Connor and me for over a year. If it's Felix and his sons who are lurking around your property, I have full confidence in your ability to defend your family."

Everett nodded and looked up at the doorway to the parlor. "Let's hope it does not come to that."

Connor lifted the deck of cards and tapped it on the table as Mandy and Lydia stepped back into the kitchen. "Anyone up for another round?"

Everett stood. "Another time perhaps. Come, Mandy, I will walk you home."

Mandy crinkled her forehead at Everett. Levi expected her to protest being ushered home by her younger brother, but she simply said her goodbyes and left with Everett.

Connor stood and carried the empty glasses to the sink, and then he turned to Lydia and caught her hand. "We should be going, too."

Levi followed them to the door and closed it behind them. He walked back to the table and put out one of the oil lamps but left the other lit for his father. The sudden silence in the house seemed unusual. He was glad his days of living there were soon to end. He stood above the kitchen table with both palms resting upon it and stared at the stone hearth around the fireplace. The stones had a hypnotic effect on him, forcing him to think of his mother—not the warm sentiment of her life but the traumatic event that led to her death. Ever since that day the house felt tainted to him. He remembered those few horrid moments vividly: he and Lydia were playing in the parlor. His mother and father were in the kitchen. Someone entered the kitchen through the back door. He heard men's voices, their volume raised in argument. Lydia ran to see what was happening and he followed her. Three angry looking strangers were rifling through the kitchen cabinets. His mother tried to stop the oldest man, and he shoved her. She fell onto the hearth and her head hit the stone. She didn't move. Lydia rushed to her. Levi envisioned his twelve-year-old self, staring up at his father, expecting him to do something to the man for that, but his father simply stood there as the men ran away.

The bitterness born in that moment still shrouded his life. He thought of the one chance he had to fight Felix since then—on the road near Northcrest when he and Connor had traveled the Land. He had not been prepared to fight then; when he recognized Felix and his sons, he had been overcome with anger and lost his focus. He thought about the campsite Everett had found and wondered if he would get another chance to fight Felix Colburn and his two sons. If he did, he determined this time Felix wouldn't get away.

* * *

Justin Mercer locked the deadbolt on the door of his room at what was once a tourist lodge near Stanley Port on East Island in the Falklands. He stepped into the bathroom with the fresh bar of soap he had spotted in the back of the hotel's looted custodial closet. Regardless of the direction he turned the faucet, the temperature of the water remained the same. After nearly a year in Antarctica, lukewarm water felt like a luxurious thermal spa. He scrubbed his hands and fingernails with passionate vigor. The only problem more daunting than starvation in the current state of the world was infection.

With the disintegration of all satellite communications for the Unified States military and most of its allies, Mercer's time in Antarctica had stretched from a three-month assignment to a yearlong nightmare. He was one of the few men at McMurdo Station on Ross Island who made it to the icebreaker in time to leave before winter. But due to the rumor of an enemy vessel in the Drake Passage, the ship stopped at Palmer Station and wintered there.

After six months at Palmer Station, with no military communication, orders or pay, he had decided the other men were right—it was every man for himself. After much persuasion, an exasperated officer of the fragmented British Forces agreed to grant him passage to the Falkland Islands in exchange for technical assistance in refitting the nuclear-powered icebreaker for military use. He no longer reported for duty and no one called him Lieutenant, but he was fortunate for the opportunity to exchange work for a room in an ally-controlled port town in one of the only places left on earth with clean drinking water.

Mercer used the soap to wash his face and then reached for the stained hand towel beside the sink. After ten hours on his back beneath a computer panel in the hull of the icebreaker, he was tired and hungry. He looked in the mirror—his black hair lashed out in every direction. The thick beard he had grown during his time in Antarctica begged for a shaving. He reminded himself of an ancient maritime sailor rather than a twenty-eight year old naval flight officer. He reached for his razor.

After shaving, Mercer dried his face then dropped the towel on the bathroom counter and walked to the rumpled bed. On his way, he picked up a file containing every note he had printed on actual paper before they lost power at McMurdo Station. Now three months out of Antarctica, he still grappled to find a way to get back to the uncharted land he had spotted after being ejected from a fighter jet nearly two years before. Every piece of information he had about that mysterious land in the South Atlantic Ocean was in the file he held.

Perched on the edge of the bed, Mercer flipped through the file's pages. Though no actual image of the land ever appeared on the satellite feeds he had closely monitored, he held several printouts of data indicating slight atmospheric discrepancies over the precise location. An occasional glance at those readings was all it took to bolster his faith in the existence of a pure and peaceful land. His focus on finding that land had thus far sustained his will to survive and still gave him hope that one day he would fulfill the innate desire for a peaceful life. The war had left a world devoid of hope, and he would have succumbed to the same despair as everyone else if he had not spotted that one piece of uncharted land.

During his winter in Antarctica, Mercer had determined he would to do whatever it took to return to those coordinates at sea and confirm with his own eyes the land existed. If his plan with the repurposed icebreaker worked, he could be on his way to the coordinates within weeks.

As he began to replay a favorite fantasy of his new life on the uncharted land, a knock at the door jarred him from his mental theater. A fish-eyed glimpse through the peephole revealed an unknown man with spiky gray hair, thin arms covered in faded tattoos, and a triangular patch of whiskers below his bottom lip. The man knocked a second time. Mercer kept the chain locked on the door and slipped his hand around his back to the loaded sidearm tucked into the waistband of his pants. With the other hand he unlocked the deadbolt and cracked the door. "Who are you?"

"Can I come in?" The skin of the man's forehead looked like leather, and his Commonwealth accent hinted at a South African origin.

"No. What do you want?" Mercer had mastered the petulant tone of the war-torn world.

"Are you Mercer?"

"Who are you?"

"I'll not say out here."

"You'll stay out there unless you say."

The man leaned close to the crack in the door. "If you're Mercer, I know about the land you're looking for."

Mercer pulled back—not only from the rancid combination of garlic and alcohol on the man's breath, but also from shock. He had not mentioned the uncharted land to anyone since he was at McMurdo Station months before. "What land?"

The man snickered and looked down. "The land you saw after you and your mate crashed in twenty twenty-five." His barely audible voice drew Mercer back to the crack in the door. "If you're still looking for that land, I might be able to assist your efforts."

"What's in it for you?"

The man's gaze shot to Mercer's. He looked serious and desperate. "A chance to get off this disease-infested island before I'm hacking up blood like the rest of these poor buggers."

Mercer closed the door with a dull thud. He swallowed hard and slid the flaking brass chain off the door. The chain dangled from its screw in the doorframe and swung a couple of times while he paused with his hand on the doorknob. He couldn't operate the ship without a crew, so he opened the door.

The man stepped into Mercer's room and scanned the space with rapid eye movements. He stood several inches shorter than Mercer and wore a sweatband on one wrist. "They call me Volt."

Mercer recognized the name but had never seen the man in person. Volt's reputation for technological and seafaring genius contradicted his washed-up beach-punk appearance. Mercer closed the door then locked the chain and the deadbolt. "I've heard of you. What's your real name?"

Volt's eyes shifted to the side and then back to Mercer. "I haven't given a real name since o-eight when my freshman hacking skills ticked off the Maritime Bureau."

Mercer lifted his papers from the bed, closed the file, and motioned with it to a wicker chair near the foot of the bed. The chair's cane creaked when Volt sat down. Mercer sat on the edge of the bed and stared at the infamous mariner. He thought Volt looked more like a man who would sleep at a beachside bus stop between stints in court-ordered rehab than a man known for outsmarting the best navy captains on the high seas.

Volt pointed at the manila file folder in Mercer's hand. "Is that your location proof?"

Mercer wasn't sure he appreciated Volt's knowledge of his work. He tucked the folder beneath his leg. "How do you know about me?"

Volt laced his fingers behind his head and leaned against the high back of the wicker chair. "A bloke at the pub in town claimed he was at McMurdo with a

Yank jet jockey who was obsessed with some uncharted land in the middle of the South Atlantic. The bloke had a few in him and mouthed off about the emergency eject that sent you just close enough to paradise to make you crazy."

Mercer smirked at hearing himself described that way. "So what—you came to hear my crazy story for yourself?"

Volt shook his head. "The thing is—I already knew about your work. You spent months observing the coordinates through the secure satellite network." When Mercer simply glared, Volt shrugged. "I linked into the monitoring unit the U.S. Navy left at the rescue site. It was part of a previous engagement."

"Let me guess… you're responsible for taking out the entire ally satellite communications networks."

Volt raised both palms. "I'll neither confirm nor deny my employment contracts, mate. The important thing is—I noticed your work and when I heard that bloke at the pub, I made some inquiries to find you."

"Because you want off this disease-infected island?"

"That's half of it."

"Here we go." Mercer wiped a hand over his freshly shaven face. "What's the other half? I don't have some Swiss bank account you can run dry, so what could you possibly gain from helping me find the land?"

"I want the same thing you want—a chance to live in peace."

"I find that hard to believe." Mercer stood. He paced to the window but kept his eyes on Volt. He didn't trust Volt, but if he was going to make it to the coordinates, he had to trust someone at some point. He studied the man called Volt—stupid moniker, but he did have a reputation. "If I did believe you, what could you do to get us there?"

Volt grinned, emitting the kind of satisfaction he should have known to conceal. He leaned forward resting his elbows on his knees. "You've got access to the ship—I can get the ship to the coordinates without being caught."

"What ship?"

Volt narrowed his eyes. "Come on, mate, you know it has crossed your mind."

He knew exactly what Volt meant—the thought of stealing the icebreaker had more than crossed his mind—it was his plan. However, assembling an able crew willing to commit to that level of idiocy was another thing. Since it appeared Volt already knew everything about him, Mercer decided to level with him. He returned to his seat on the edge of the bed. "How do we get a crew, steal a nuclear-powered icebreaker, and cruise to the middle of the South Atlantic without being caught?"

"The Brits sent for a commercial cruise ship that has been sitting at South Georgia Island since the war began. They plan to take everyone they can fit aboard to Valparaiso. There is a warehouse in Santiago full of antibiotics that the Royal Forces are guarding to treat their own. I figured since you have access to the icebreaker for your work on the refit, you simply stall the work until they are gone."

"The refit is almost complete. The ship is ready and they know it. How am I supposed to stall?"

"Simple. We program a false reading with a coolant warning on the reactor's power output information display. There's no way they will put her into service. And with no fuel available for the back-up diesel engines, she will sit in the dock indefinitely. Then the cruise ship will arrive to take everyone to Valparaiso and... bam!" Volt clapped. "We've got ourselves a free ship with the potential to stay at sea fully-powered for a year, maybe more."

Impressed with the plan, Mercer nodded. "The technical manuals are onboard—"

Volt waved a hand. "I don't need manuals."

"I do." Securing the ship was only the first challenge. He didn't know how they would operate the nuclear-powered ship once they had it. "What kind of crew do we need?"

"A skeleton crew for that ship would consist of twelve men, fourteen tops. I've got six picked out already."

"Have you spoken to them about this?"

"Not yet. It's too soon."

Mercer liked what he heard, but still thought it sounded too easy. Volt seemed to know everything about him and already had more than half of the crew ready. A man with his expertise could easily get past security codes and steal the icebreaker by himself if he wanted to. Volt didn't need him, so Mercer thought it had to be a set-up. His suspicion returned with intensity. He glared at Volt. "What are you really after? You want my room or something? I don't get it—do you leave here and tell my C.O. and I lose my job?"

"You don't have a C.O. anymore. Military command is obsolete. The guys at the dock are leaving. I'm not staying here and I'm not going to die in Chile. Of all the jobs I've done in the past two decades, this is the one that finally ends with me in paradise. Considering what is out there, this is my last chance. It's yours, too." Volt leaned forward. "Sure, I could bypass the security codes and take the ship myself, but after I heard about your experience, I thought you'd be anxious for a lift. If you can fly a jet, you can master that ship, no worries."

Mercer knew it was probably his only chance. He needed someone like Volt to make it happen and if he refused, Volt would probably take the ship anyway. Mercer stood and pushed a hand through his shaggy hair. "Fine. Get your crew together. I'll stall the work."

CHAPTER FOUR

The late afternoon sun cast Mandy's shadow long and angled beside her as she walked on the cobblestone street through the village of Good Springs. She unbuttoned the second button of her dress, eliciting a scowling glance from an older village woman. The oppressive heat made her indifferent to traditional modesty. Despite her upbringing, her behavior sometimes escaped the limits of cultural propriety. Shifting her encased violin in front of her body to carry it in the other hand, she decided she would reschedule her music students to cooler morning hours for the remainder of the summer.

As she walked toward home, she imagined idling the evening away in her family's farmhouse wishing for relief from the heat. The image stirred a hollow, lonely feeling and compelled her to defer the final mile of her walk home. She wiped her sweaty palm on her yellow summer dress and looked for company. It would be the perfect afternoon to spend at the springs north of the village. The thought of floating in the cool fresh water made her hum. It was a shame the springs were simply too far away to walk to in this heat.

Her thick ponytail of curls flopped as she turned her head from side to side, scanning the empty porches in the village. The rare heat spell always seemed to have a vacating effect on Good Springs, and she detested it. As she passed the pottery yard, she felt a wave of relief when she spotted Bethany Colburn.

Mandy stopped near the short wooden fence in front of the pottery yard and greeted the owner. "Good afternoon, Mrs. Vestal." The top-heavy woman responded with a nod then wiped her face with her sleeve as she lumbered under an open shelter and sat at her pottery wheel.

Dimples pitted Bethany's cheeks as she smiled and walked across the sandy yard toward the gate. Her work dress was speckled with pigments and flecks of dried clay. Mandy lifted the latch on a short gate and held it open for Bethany. "Are you on your way home?"

"Yes, Mrs. Vestal said it's time for me to go, but I really could have worked until nightfall and been content." Bethany stepped through the gate carrying a large pot in each arm. The pots were identical in shape and form but different in color. "I'm taking these home to paint the finishing details. What do you think of the glaze?"

Mandy understood the desire for affirmation innate in every artist, but she still thought of Bethany less as a craftsman and more as the youngest of the Colburn children. To Mandy, Bethany would forever be her best friend's baby sister. She sighed at the notion of Bethany growing up and gave the pots a quick visual examination. "It is unusual. I like it."

They walked away from the pottery yard together and shuffled down the road. Mandy slowed their pace because the heat stunted her energy. Bethany chatted about her pottery work as they walked. "I made the pigment from a new mix of minerals I'm experimenting with. I think the best way to achieve a quality finish is to grind the minerals in a mortar before boiling down the glaze, but Mrs. Vestal says until my apprenticeship is complete, I must follow her procedure. What do you think of the colors?"

Mandy glanced again at the pots in Bethany's arms. The waning sunlight refracted through the glaze and caused a fluid luminescence. "I can honestly say I've never seen anything like it. You're truly a gifted artist." She looked up at Bethany—almost seventeen and full of passion for her craft. With her defined features and long legs, she looked like a woman on the outside, though her trusting and unaffected nature betrayed her childlike naiveté. Still, she was company—even if it was only as far as the Colburn property.

Mandy shifted her gaze back to the road. In the distance, Everett was walking toward the village, probably on his way to spar with Connor. Mandy imagined Levi would join them later. The thought of men training for physical violence excited her, though their reasons were practical in nature.

She understood the familiarity between her younger brother and Bethany and held a secret hope their friendship would blossom into something more one day. She kept her eyes on Everett's distant figure, but turned her chin to Bethany. "Do you and Everett get to see each other very often now that he has completed school?"

Bethany's pink cheeks—still cushioned with youth—rose as she smiled. "He comes by the pottery yard occasionally to visit me." She giggled, displaying her lingering juvenile tendencies. "Why? Do you know something?"

"No, just curious." Mandy grinned. The temptation to meddle stewed beneath her surface as she watched Everett walk nearer on the road. "I suppose he's on his way to see Connor today."

"Yes, probably. He spars with Connor and Levi every week. I'm not allowed near the barn when they are in there, though sometimes when I know they are fighting, I feel desperate with curiosity." She giggled again, then seriousness marked her expression. "Please, don't tell Lydia I said that."

"Of course not." Mandy felt wicked but enjoyed the similarities between her nature and Bethany's too much to care. "If I were you, I would be curious too."

Bethany began to talk about the curiosities of male behavior—a subject in which Mandy considered herself an expert—but two men riding horseback farther down the road caught her attention. She wondered who they could be, but they were still too far away to see their features through the dusty air.

The riders moved behind Everett on the road. They directed their horses around him and passed him by. She continued to watch them as she and Bethany left the road near the Colburn property and walked through the cut grass toward the house. As the men rode closer, her boredom stirred her desire for attention and she smiled with alluring intent in their direction. Soon she got a clear look at their faces and immediately regretted her flirtation. Though she didn't recognize the men, their strange features and hungry expressions endowed them with a sinister quality she instinctively knew to evade. Her smile vanished and she hurried Bethany across the Colburn property. "Move along, Bethany."

"Whatever for?" Bethany began to giggle then stopped as she looked in the direction of the oncoming riders. Her face changed and she stood still. "Who are they?"

"I don't know, but you must come along." She pulled at Bethany's elbow as she heard the horses' gait increase in speed and proximity. It filled her with trepidation. Bethany gulped audibly, but she didn't move. The riders were coming straight at them, and Mandy felt the overwhelming need to protect Bethany. "Go to the house, Bethany. Quickly!"

The earth beneath Mandy's feet rumbled with the close and heavy thumps of the hooves and, before she could look back, the men were on either side of her. One rider bent from his saddle and grabbed her with both hands. The sound of smashing pottery told her the other man must have grabbed Bethany in the same way.

The man's hard fingers dug into her flesh, forcing a scream from her throat. She dropped her encased violin and swung her arms in a panicked fight as the man hoisted her from the ground. He pulled her up by the shoulders and smashed her onto the saddle, pressing her body with his weight. She was bent at the middle over the animal, and her lungs gushed out air from the pressure of the saddle horn against her chest. She heard Bethany's screams, Everett's shouting voice, and a horse's neigh in the distance as her captor rode quickly away with her restrained in front of him on the horse.

Mandy's vision blurred from the jarring motion as her face was compressed against the horse's moving shoulder. She grabbed at the straps and the side of the saddle, but her fingers felt numb and couldn't get a grip on anything. She tried to hang on and lift her weight off her strained ribcage. The man leaned his elbows into her spine, subduing her every effort. She tried to scream but couldn't get enough air into her lungs without it being jarred back out again. The gravel of the road blurred, and if they kept going in that direction they would soon pass Levi's property—maybe he would see her and stop this madman from his brutal attack. If Levi saw her, he could save her before she fell to her death or before this miscreant took her somewhere and did whatever he planned to do. Knowing they would soon pass Levi's property, she gathered the air to scream, but the horse leapt and the green pasture of her family's farm blurred beneath its hooves. The horse didn't slow its pace for what felt like a torturous eternity across the empty pasture. Her body writhed with pain and she fought to remain conscious. With every passing second, she gave up hope for being seen by anyone who could help her. Then the horse slowed to a stop and the man's arms came off her back. She slid her hands beneath her chest and gasped for air. She heard wheezing and realized the sound was coming from her breath. With her hair hanging in her face, she lifted her head. She saw rocks, the edges of which distorted in her vision. She squeezed her eyes shut and blinked them open again. The boulder outcrops and creek were at the western edge of her family's property, far from the village and her family and any chance of being heard and saved.

Before her captor dismounted, someone grabbed her and pulled her from the horse. She was dropped to her feet and spun around with force by a middle-aged man. He had a kinked moustache that curled into his mouth. His black and silver hair draped over his shoulders. Gripping both of her wrists, he studied her and then turned his face toward her abductor. "You got a pretty one, son. But she don't look like no Colburn woman to me."

Mandy's red curls stuck to her sweaty face, obscuring her view. She drew a breath then lifted her leg and stomped on the older man's foot. "Let me go!" she demanded, but he barely flinched. Panting, she struggled to pull her hands loose, but the strength of her tired arms was no match for the nefarious-looking man.

Both men stood close together and examined her. Frantic, she shifted her gaze from one man to the other. The men looked alike except for a twenty-year difference. And they both seemed pleased with themselves.

When she tried to pull her hands away again, the older man laughed. "She's spirited! We've never had one this feisty, have we, Harvey? There's only one way to break a woman like her." He let go of her wrists, and immediately the man he called Harvey stepped close and grinned.

Mandy's pulse pounded in her ears. She scurried backward into the boulders and scanned the space around her for a way of escape but saw none. Harvey appeared amused by her panic. He grabbed the back of her neck and parted his crackled lips. She sucked in every inch of air she could and screamed until her voice burned. Harvey pulled back then angled his head and chuckled.

"Silence your woman and get her in the wagon!" the older man yelled.

"Let me break her first, Father."

"Not now. Get her into the wagon so we can leave."

Harvey wrapped his fingers through the bulk of Mandy's hair and jerked her toward a covered wagon. "But I think we should wait here for Christopher," Harvey protested, speaking of the other rider—the one who attacked Bethany.

"Did he get a woman too?"

"Yes, his woman has brown hair and she's real tall. I wanted this one because she smiled at me. Once she settles down a bit, I think we'll get along just fine." Harvey gripped her arms and pushed her up into the back of the wagon. "Christopher should be here in a few minutes. I want to wait for him."

"We can't wait—the sun will be down soon and we aren't going to stay this close to the village tonight. Christopher knows where to meet us. Get in the back of the wagon with that woman and keep her quiet."

In the back of the foul-smelling covered wagon, Mandy curled her legs into her chest. Her body ached. Her mind reeled knowing Bethany had also been captured. Bethany was so young and innocent—she didn't deserve to be attacked. Mandy would find a way to deal with what came to her, but Bethany still had a chance at life and love.

Harvey sat by the opening at the back of the wagon. Mandy thought about trying to push around him and jump out once it started rolling. Then she thought of Bethany and decided to wait. She didn't want Bethany left alone with these men all night. She would be there for Bethany when she arrived and they would escape their captors together.

* * *

Levi drew a line across a plank of gray leaf wood marking where to make a cut. Then he wedged his pencil over his ear and carried the marked board out of his unfinished house. He steadied the plank with one hand and gripped his saw with the other. The quick sounds made by the saw blade's teeth as it cut through the wood swished until the board fell in two. As he reached to the ground to pick up the wood, a little yellow daisy in the grass caught his eye. He brushed the sawdust from his hands and picked the tiny flower. Unable to feel the true softness of the fragile petals through the calloused skin of his fingertips, he lightly traced the flower along the sensitive scar on his palm. Then he dropped the flower, picked up the piece of wood, and walked back into the house. After he nailed the board into place, he slid his hammer through his belt and walked to a wide window opening. Instead of the constant ocean breeze that usually moved over his hill and through the shell of a house, stagnant air hung humid and limp around his body. He pulled a handkerchief from his back pocket and wiped his face with the already damp cloth.

The rare and stifling heat left him drained at the end of the day. He walked through the house to a bucket of warm water and dipped a cup deep inside. After emptying the cup with three swallows, he drew a second cup. As he lifted it to his lips, he heard a horse riding onto his property.

He descended the steps of what would soon be his front porch and met Everett in the yard. The young man's eyes were wide and frightened. He rode a tall, black horse and pulled it to a stop in front of Levi. Everett began to speak but his voice was drowned by the horse's neigh. The horse stomped nervously. Levi grabbed its headstall to control its movement as he tried to decipher Everett's words.

"Did you see them?" Everett glanced toward the road then back at Levi.

"Who?"

"The man who took Mandy."

"What man? Who took Mandy?"

"One of the men…" Everett held the reins in one hand and wiped his forehead with the other. "There were two men on the road. Did you see them?"

"No one has passed here in hours." He noticed Everett's hands were shaking. "What has happened?"

Everett swung down from the horse. He handed the reins to Levi and propped his knuckles on his knees while he caught his breath. When he lifted his head again, his eyes were red and swollen. "I was on my way to spar with Connor and I was on the road and I saw Bethany and Mandy walking toward your house—or, your family's house. Two riders came from behind me on the road. They quickly passed me and went straight for the girls." His voice trembled as he spoke. "One man grabbed Mandy and the other grabbed Bethany. I ran as fast as I could and I got Bethany before he could pull her onto the horse. He came down after her and fell under his horse's hooves. Bethany is fine, but Mandy is gone."

"Gone?" Levi realized the seriousness of Everett's report and anger surged along with his increasing pulse. "Where?"

"I don't know. I jumped on this horse and tried to follow but I lost them."

"They haven't passed here. They must have left the road."

Everett straightened his back and pushed both hands through his dark hair. "What should I do? He has my sister!"

"Go tell your father." Levi mounted the black horse. "Where is the injured man?"

"Lydia is with him."

"Alone?" Without waiting for a response, he turned the horse to the road and tore out of his property. He dug his heels into the horse's flanks, urging it to gallop until he reached the Colburn house. Guilt deluged his system as he regretted his decision to leave the family home. He should have been there to protect his young sister. He had sensed there would be trouble when he heard someone had camped near the Fosters' property. He should have done something about it before they had a chance to attack. He should have watched the road while he was building or—better yet—never have left home at all.

He leapt down from the horse between the main house and Lydia's cottage. John Colburn stood outside the back door of the family home with Bethany wrapped in his arms. She wept violently with her eyes clenched shut. Levi dropped the reins and darted for Lydia's cottage. He threw the door open and came within an inch of hitting Connor with it. Lydia stood near her patient and jumped at the commotion.

"Where is he?" Levi demanded even as his eyes landed on the insentient man sprawled on the patient cot. The man's head was swollen to one side with a purple bulge. A slow stream of blood trickled from his ear canal. Levi instantly recognized the injured man. "That's Felix's son! I knew it! I will kill him!" He lunged toward the patient cot, but Connor held him back.

Lydia snapped her head at Connor. "Get him out of here!"

"I'm not leaving you alone with him," Connor yelled at Lydia. He kept a grip on Levi but it was half-hearted and Levi knew it. Both men wanted her patient dead, but Lydia's sworn duty imposed a standard on them that required unmitigated self-control. "He will die." Connor lowered his voice as if to give Levi a covert message. "Save your anger for Felix."

Levi shook his shoulders away from Connor and stomped to the open door. "Where is the other one? The one who has Mandy?" Before Connor answered, Levi blew out a breath and punched his fist into the doorframe. "I will find her. I will kill Felix... and his son. I will kill them both."

Levi looked out at Bethany, who was clinging to their father. He wanted to comfort her, but he didn't want to take a step outside of Lydia's office as long as Felix's son was still breathing. He also wanted to find Mandy and kill the man who took her. His nerves quivered as much with anger as dread. Bethany opened her crying eyes, and when they met Levi's she let go of her father and rushed to Levi. She buried her face into his neck and sobbed. It sickened Levi to think of anyone harming his little sister. He pressed his lips to the top of her head. "Are you hurt?"

"Not really. Not like Mandy." She pulled back and looked at Levi. "The other man took her. Everett tried to follow them." Her blue eyes were encircled by red from weeping. The striking contrast tore at his racing heart.

"I know. Everett came to me. He lost them."

John moved close to them. "Where is Everett now?"

"I sent him to his parents." Levi looked at his father and suddenly felt like a child again—like the twelve-year-old boy who had watched Felix push his mother into the hearth. His jaw ached from grinding his teeth. "We must do something, Father."

John nodded then looked past Levi's shoulder into the cottage. "Connor, stay here with Lydia. Don't let her out of your sight."

"Yes, sir."

"I will keep Bethany with me." John reached for her and Levi opened his arms to let her go. "Levi, I want you to go to the Fosters. I know Everett is

distraught, but I want you to devise a plan with him—
a way to protect the village. Be strong for Samuel and
Roseanna, son."

Levi didn't think that was much of a plan. He
drew in a slow breath through flared nostrils. Connor
was the only man among them ever to engage in
battle, and his opinion meant more to Levi than any
other. Levi looked back at Connor, needing a visual
cue confirming John's orders. Connor seemed to
understand and nodded once at him. Levi looked at
Bethany one last time. She was safe now, though he
had not been the one to protect her—Everett had. And
now Everett was the one missing a sister.

The black horse grazed in the yard, indifferent to
all the chaos. As Levi took the reins and raised
himself to the saddle, he realized this was one of the
two horses hitched to his father's wagon when Felix
and his sons stole it on the road near Northcrest two
years prior. Lydia had given those horses to Levi as a
gift and—though he had not owned the horses long—
he knew this was one of them. His emotions coursed
with such explosive anger over Mandy's abduction
they left no room to enjoy the satisfaction of getting
his horse back.

He squeezed the horse's barrel with his heels,
sending it into a gallop. Dirt and gravel flew behind
them on the road. Even as the sun's last light faded,
he wanted to keep riding until he found Mandy. He
considered getting Everett and searching for any
tracks diverging from the road before it was too dark.
He also considered riding to every property around
the village to make inquires—perhaps someone saw
something. But his father had said to comfort the

Fosters and devise a plan. Connor had agreed, but it didn't feel like enough to Levi. His compunction over the attack grew every second. He had to do something.

Levi rode to the Fosters' farmhouse and let himself in the front door. He found Everett and Samuel and Roseanna huddled together in their front parlor, weeping. As an elder in the village, Samuel Foster was a figure of strength and wisdom. But Levi could see his own father was right: in the wake of the traumatic abduction of their daughter, the Fosters needed someone else to be strong.

The wooden floor in the Fosters' kitchen creaked as Levi paced the room. Everett walked into the kitchen and lowered himself into a seat at the table. His brow was tightly knit as Roseanna continued to weep from the sorrowful shock. Eventually, her sobs lessened to whimpers. Finally, she lifted her head from Samuel's shoulder. She stepped into the kitchen and went straight to the sink. Samuel remained in the parlor, staring out the window into the blackened night.

Levi glanced out the kitchen window to the west. He felt desperate to search for Mandy, but it would be futile at night without even knowing in what direction they went. He wanted to jump on the horse and ride until he found her, but he wouldn't be able to track them in the dark and it would be unwise to set out alone. Felix's sons had not plotted this on their own, so there would be at least two men out there to fight. Levi felt confident he could handle both men, but his attention would be divided if he were also trying to free Mandy.

He remembered his father's instruction to devise a plan and decided that plan shouldn't be to protect the village but to search for Mandy and kill her abductor and Felix. He pulled a chair away from the table and sat across from Everett. "We should start with the campsite you found."

Everett leaned forward. "Do you think it's the same men?"

"Yes. It's Felix Colburn and his sons. The wagon tracks you saw at the campsite were probably from my father's old wagon—they took it when they attacked Connor and me two years ago."

Everett straightened his posture and crossed his arms over his chest. "Connor has taught us to fight. We could easily overpower them—you and I—and save my sister."

"I want Connor with us."

"Your father won't allow all three of us to leave the village. He will want Connor to stay for Lydia's sake."

Levi knew Everett was right. "There are only two of them now—Connor said the man in Lydia's office will die from his injuries. The three of us could take care of the problem once and for all. They can't get away with this. They deserve to be punished and we're the only men willing to deliver justice."

He looked up as Samuel stepped into the kitchen from the parlor. Samuel had his hand over his heart as he lowered himself into a chair at the table. "Are you boys going to search for Mandy?"

Everett shifted in his seat and turned to his father. "Yes, but we want Connor to go with us."

Samuel nodded, then his eyes moved to Levi. "Did you get a look at Bethany's attacker?"

"Yes. He is Felix's son."

"Then there are still two demons out there." Samuel rubbed his forehead with his thumb. "And they have my Mandy."

"Father," Everett's jaw bulged as he clenched his teeth. "I'm sorry I didn't save Mandy." He looked at Levi then. "I'm not sorry I saved Bethany... I just wish I could've saved them both."

Levi glanced at Samuel and saw his chin quiver beneath his white beard. He understood Everett's dejection. "You saved my sister and I'm grateful, Everett. I'm sorry I wasn't there. I can't tell you how sorry, but our regrets won't help us find Mandy."

"When I do find them..." Everett pounded his fist onto the table's surface. "I am going to tear that man's head from his body. I am going to—"

"Enough, son." Samuel raised his palm, silencing Everett's angry words. "Your fury will serve you well when it's time to fight. Let your love for your sister and for justice drive you into that battle."

Everett pressed his lips together and nodded. It was a wonder he was able to control himself at all. Mandy had been stolen. Felix and his sons had to die. Levi stood from the table and paced to the window as his aggression surged. He craved the battle, not simply for the potential of serving justice, but also for the pleasure of releasing years of anger over his mother's death.

Samuel looked at him. "You too, Levi. Focus on the task at hand and keep anger in its place. Come sit back down." Levi returned to the table out of respect for Samuel. After a moment, Samuel rapped his knuckles on the table. "Very well, then. I have maps of the westward property. We will need them to plan your search."

CHAPTER FIVE

The night air remained warm and thick. Every sash window in the Fosters' farmhouse gaped at the darkness. Roseanna Foster stood at the kitchen sink scrubbing one spot of the porcelain basin with abandon. The scratching sound of her scrub brush paused occasionally as she lifted her wrist to dab her tears with her sleeve. Levi had never witnessed such anxiety from the usually cheerful matron, and he prayed she would be reunited with Mandy soon.

Samuel emerged from the hallway clutching a bundle of rolled-up papers. He sat beside Everett and unfurled the documents on the table, revealing hand-drawn maps. Levi began to examine them from across the table when the sound of voices outside caught his attention. He left the table and walked to the front parlor just as Connor opened the door from the outside. John, Bethany, and Lydia followed Connor into the house. Connor was holding Mandy's violin case. He set it on the floor of the parlor as Roseanna met the women at the door. She directed them down the hallway and into Mandy's bedroom, where their collective weeping swelled into a cacophony of grief.

John and Connor walked to the table. John pulled out the chair next to Samuel and sat. "Bethany's attacker is dead. Lydia said there was nothing she could do for him. I believe he was the younger of Felix's two sons—if so, his name was Christopher Colburn." John looked down at his hands as he brushed his fingertips together. "Felix's other son is named Harvey."

Levi's anger flared as John announced Mandy's attacker's name. He stretched his neck deep to one side, then the other, and repeated the name with a barely audible growl, wondering how his father knew the names of Felix's sons. He decided to focus his attention on finding Mandy as Samuel had suggested.

Levi returned to his seat and motioned to the empty chair next to him for Connor. Samuel shook his head somberly and turned his attention back to his maps. Connor pointed to the faded maps spread across the kitchen table. "Is this a map of your property, Mr. Foster?"

"And the area beyond my property." Samuel cleared his throat, but his voice remained gruff as he traced his finger along the ancient paper. "The western edge of my land is bounded by this creek—it would probably be shallow this time of year. I haven't ventured far beyond that point, but my father occasionally did. He drew this map of the pine forest and the simplest route to the river from there."

Connor glanced at Levi. "Is that where you think Felix and Harvey are taking her?"

Levi nodded and pulled another map from the stack. The heavy papers crackled as they slid over the table. He looked at his father and motioned to different aspects of the map. "We think they came from here—near the mountains to the west. If they came to Good Springs to steal women, they were probably planning to return this way. Everett said he saw wagon tracks at the campsite he found last week on the western edge of the property here. The closest bridge over the river is here—about thirty miles from Good Springs."

John leaned back in his chair and raised an eyebrow as he looked at the map. Levi judged his father's demeanor as one of barely-cloaked superiority and thought such confidence was unwelcome in the situation no matter how much undisclosed information his father held. Maybe Connor—with his military experience—would have a right to exude such confidence, but not his father. The man had never fought anyone in his life.

John shook his head, disagreeing with Levi's assessment of the attacker's plan. "Felix does not yet know Christopher is dead. He won't go home. He will wait nearby for his son."

The quick dismissal of Levi's opinion stoked the fire of his already burning anger. He glowered at his father. "How do you know what Felix will do?"

"Because I am a father!" John shoved back from the table and stood. He paced to the window and pushed his hands through his hair. Levi watched his father and felt no less angry but was pleased the impudent question had elicited such an outburst.

When John didn't turn back to them, Levi glanced at the other men. Everett looked at his hands. Connor tapped one finger on the edge of the table.

Samuel stared at John's back, stunned by the overseer's loss of control.

Levi studied Samuel for longer than he intended, and all at once Samuel seemed old to him. He had always thought of Samuel as fatherly but never as elderly. Perhaps it was the dread of the situation that cast shadows through the creases around Samuel's eyes, leaving him sallow. His shoulders slumped, aging him even more.

Samuel looked at Levi but angled his head toward John. "John, you can keep guard over your house and I can keep guard over mine in case Felix does come back, but I think the boys should go and search for Mandy." Samuel pulled his lips tightly together as he struggled not to weep. "You are the overseer and I will respect whatever you think is best for the village. Please, send the boys to search for my daughter—my precious daughter."

John stepped behind Samuel and put both hands on his shoulders in support. Everett dropped his face into his hands, and Connor blew out a breath through pursed lips. Samuel's palpable agony filled the room. Levi felt it and thought his own pain was only marginally less as he waited for John's response.

"Levi, Connor, Everett—you will depart at first light." John's jaw was tight as he gave the orders. "Take the horses and whatever provisions you need. Begin with the campsite to the west and look for tracks. Stay together. Find Amanda and bring her home."

Everett lifted his face from his hands. Connor leaned forward and pulled the maps close to examine them. Levi's anger shifted away from his father and back to the man who took Mandy.

* * *

Mandy remained curled in a protective ball beside her abductor in the back of the wagon as the older man drove them westward through the night. She tried not to look at Harvey, but she felt him leering at her through the darkness. Her body ached; every muscle and sinew felt torn from the attack. She wondered how she would fight whenever Harvey finally decided to make his move.

The wagon jerked hard and then swayed, throwing Mandy closer to Harvey. She sucked in a breath and jumped back against the wagon's side. When he did nothing, she wondered if he were asleep. She relaxed her arms but kept them wrapped around her legs.

Harvey sniffed and shifted his position. She froze, hoping not to wake him. The wagon continued swaying as it rolled. She glanced through the small opening at the front of the wagon cover and saw the back of the older man's head and the blackness of the sky beyond.

Harvey moved again and cleared his throat. "What's your name?"

Mandy's breath came in short pulses as her fear intensified. She considered remaining silent but her intellect was her only remaining defense. She decided to find a way to use it. "Amanda Foster."

She waited with every breath to flinch at his advance but he didn't move, nor did he say anything.

After several minutes, she turned her eyes and looked in his direction. His face was blackened by the darkness inside the wagon, but she could see his silhouette.

"Foster?" His voice was barely above a whisper. "Aren't you a Colburn woman?"

"No, I am not a Colburn woman." She wondered why he thought she was a Colburn. Then she remembered she was walking with Bethany across the Colburn property when they were attacked. She couldn't understand how these men knew the Colburns of Good Springs or why they had specifically targeted women they believed to be Colburns.

The wagon rattled as it moved through the darkness. Every shake vibrated through her aching body and intensified the pain in her chest. She wondered where they were taking her and where the other attacker was and what he had done with Bethany. She wanted the wagon to stop but also feared when it did stop she would be forced to endure something much worse.

Harvey breathed heavily several times, his nose whistling with each exhalation. "Don't tell my father."

"Don't tell him what?" Her throat burned when she spoke.

"Don't tell him that you aren't a Colburn."

"Why not?"

"He'll be mad at me."

She sensed a chance to angle between the men and decided to test their fortitude. "Why would he be angry with you?"

Harvey snorted, putting an end to his nasal whistle. "Father says since we are Colburns we should have Colburn women. Don't tell him you aren't a Colburn."

She thought of the well-instilled custom of recording genealogy to avoid inbreeding in the Land and wondered how ignorant these men were to strive for such eschewed forbidden coupling. With her intimate knowledge of the Colburn family of Good Springs and their heritage, she doubted these men were close relatives of John Colburn.

She tried to think of a way to use Harvey's request to secure her freedom and considered using charm, but that would only encourage him. The last thing she wanted to do was to elicit desire. Instead, she tempered her voice. "Why should I help you?"

"Because you're my wife."

"I am not your wife!"

"I will make you my wife." His voice grew closer. "As soon as Father says I can."

Mandy locked her arms around her curled legs. "You cannot."

"Why not?"

"Because I... I have women's troubles... and if you touch me it will cause your manhood to shrivel." She didn't care if she breached custom by speaking of something indecorous to a man. Nor did she care that she had uttered a complete lie. She only cared that he believed her lie and was as repulsed as she intended for him to be.

Harvey was silent. He returned to his place by the back of the wagon. She heard nothing else from him the remainder of the night aside from snoring.

Eventually she loosened the grip of her arms and tried to shift her legs, but she never slept.

The pain in her chest kept her mind alert. Though she was injured in body and trapped in a wagon that smelled like rancid meat, she tried to think of something else. She focused her thoughts on her family and imagined her mother in the kitchen—not scrubbing frantically like she did when she was nervous, but baking happily on a Saturday afternoon. She thought of their shared humor. She remembered what it felt like to lay her head in her mother's lap as a child. Her mother would play with her curls while they listened to her father tell stories by the fireplace. It pained her to think of her father because he would have wept when he learned of her abduction. Mother cried easily because that is what mothers do. But when Father cried it meant something truly terrible had happened. She didn't want to be the subject of something truly terrible, but she was. Even if she somehow made it home, the stench of tragedy would linger on her and her family long after the details of the event had been forgotten. Even Everett would be affected. She thought of Everett then and prayed he had been able to save Bethany. She knew her brother loved Bethany and assumed he was only waiting for her to mature to declare his love. She hoped he would still do that and go on to live a happy life and have a family and take care of their parents—even if she never returned home.

She thought of Levi—though the reason her mind regarded him as family evaded her. She loved all of the Colburns, having grown up in their home as much as her own. Her closeness to Lydia should have evoked thoughts of their friendship, but she thought first of Levi. Of all the men who had been intrigued with her—and some of them had even asked her to marry—he never seemed to recover from her refusal to court. He seemed stuck in that moment ever since. It probably didn't help that her friendship with Lydia kept her in close proximity to him through the years. She did her best to ignore his surly reminders of her refusal, which often made it difficult to enjoy his company. Still, she loved him. Perhaps it was only a familial attachment, but she loved him nonetheless. If she lived through this ordeal and escaped her captors, she would show kindness to him—maybe even apologize for the hurt her refusal had caused him— not to encourage his romantic affections—she could never marry anyone—but to make things right somehow.

* * *

Levi helped Connor remove the corpse from Lydia's medical office. They covered the body in burlap and carried it to a shed at the edge of the Colburn property. John said they had enough work to do, and he and Samuel would bury the body in the village cemetery in the morning.

Levi and Connor readied their provisions for the search and walked their horses into the Fosters' barn where they met Everett. With only a few hours left until daylight, the three men slept in the loft of the barn, keeping their bodies in minimal comfort to ensure an early rise.

Levi remained awake during those hours. From where he lay in the open loft, he could see the doorway to Mandy's workshop. He thought of the instruments she built there and her skill in crafting them. He had never thought much about her work—only how erratic her work ethic seemed to be. She would go months without making any new instruments—no matter how many requests she received—then she would be in her workshop late into the night, day after day for weeks. He had judged her as capricious, but now with her gone—possibly forever—he regretted that judgment.

With each passing hour, his remorse increased. He had been in love with Mandy when he was seventeen—every unmarried male in the village was. The tomboyish redhead had grown into a stunning vixen and, due to the closeness of their families, he had felt confident she would be his. He remembered the great shock and mortification her rejection brought him, especially in consideration of the way her effusive flirtation had suggested a different outcome. Since then she acted as if his declaration of undying love had never happened, which only magnified the ache within him. She had grown more beautiful over the years, and he both longed for her attention and detested her batting eyes.

Levi reclined into the dusty haystack behind him and realized he should have spent the past six years appreciating Mandy's friendship. He thought of her music and the pleasure it brought everyone who heard her perform. She taught music lessons to many of the schoolchildren, and he often heard villagers praise her joyful, patient instruction. There would be much to regret if she were lost. He felt a surge of grief inside his heart. He remembered Samuel's admonition and resolved to use his regret to make sure he found her.

The dark space inside the doorway of her workshop beckoned him. He glanced at the other men lying in the hayloft. They appeared to be asleep, so he rose and walked to the workshop, controlling the sound of his steps so as not to wake the others.

The shop door stood open, and moonlight streamed through the gaping window in the opposite wall. The room's scent was a mixture of freshly carved gray leaf wood and drying varnish—a blend he found pleasurable, though most people would not. He considered the commonality of his and Mandy's work and realized it wasn't something he had previously acknowledged.

He stepped to the cluttered workbench and sat on a wooden stool where she spent her workdays. He took a match from a shallow jar, struck it, and lit the lantern on the end of the bench. The soft light revealed the bench's dusty surface, which had been casually cleared with a straw hand brush. Glass jars filled with a variety of screws and pegs skirted the far side of the workbench. He lifted one jar and, upon inspection, decided the workspace's contents were organized in a manner only rational to its owner.

He put the jar back then crossed his arms and leaned them onto the dusty workbench. It wasn't the same as being with her, but somehow being in her space comforted him. He noticed a short piece of dowel rod on the workbench and picked it up. As he ran it through his fingertips, he thought of Mandy. One end of the pencil-thin piece of wood was carved to a sharp point. As he wondered what she had used the piece of dowel for, Everett stepped into the workshop.

Levi looked up. "Am I keeping you awake?"

"No. I won't sleep tonight."

"Nor will I."

With one hand, Everett lifted a wooden stool that was next to the wall. He carried it to the workbench and set it at the end nearest the light. He reached his hand to the lantern and turned its knob, lowering the flame's intensity.

Levi knew when to speak and when to remain silent. His inclination—especially in the company of men—was silence, and he appreciated how Everett held a similar preference, even more so as he had matured. He also understood Everett's need for reassurance in the wake of the crisis, partially because he felt the need as well. He set the dowel on the workbench and looked at Everett. "We will find her."

Everett nodded once. "I can't come home without her. It would kill my father if I did." He picked up the dowel and peered at its sharpened tip. "Lately, he has been easily fatigued—more than usual—and I don't think he has the strength to lose her. If she dies, so will he."

"We will find her."

Everett nodded again. He placed the dowel on the workbench and covered it with his hand. More silence, then Everett stood and walked back to the hayloft. Levi leaned forward and blew out the lantern's flame, but he stayed at the workbench awhile before returning to recline on the haystacks in the loft where he waited for morning light.

* * *

The men rose before dawn and, by first light, were halfway to the campsite Everett had found days before on the western portion of the Foster property. Everett quickly spotted fresh wagon tracks across the sandy soil. Connor and Levi encouraged him to lead the way. He was right—Felix and Harvey had headed west toward the bridge. By Samuel's map, they estimated the river was thirty miles away. Everett steadily increased their pace, and Levi felt certain they would be able to catch up to the men in the wagon, execute justice and return Mandy to her family.

* * *

In the morning light, Mandy saw dark streaks of bruising across her arms. She remained imprisoned in the back of the wagon with Harvey fixed between her and the gate. Through the small opening in the cover at the front of the wagon bed, she could see the back of the older man's head. He made raucous coughing and spitting sounds as he continued to drive westward.

The wagon stopped once at midmorning and Harvey jolted awake. The older man stood guard while Harvey briefly left the wagon. She listened through the canvas wagon cover and heard crows cawing, the horses exhaling, and the men relieving themselves. Then she heard footsteps approaching the wagon and the men whispering. Soon the older man leaned his head into view and gazed at her over the wagon gate. A deep crevice formed between his spiny eyebrows, and he looked away the moment their eyes met. She realized Harvey had told his father why he shouldn't copulate with her. She was satisfied that a glance at her now evoked disgust rather than desire.

The older man climbed to the front bench and Harvey clambered into the back. He moved around her to open a sack propped in the front corner of the wagon bed. He pulled two apples from the sack and held one out to her. She took the apple and Harvey went back to his place by the gate. She noticed he was careful not to touch her, confirming he believed her fallacious caution.

In the afternoon, she felt how the earth changed beneath the wagon's wheels. She wondered if they had come upon a road or simply smoother grass. Either way, they had traveled a great distance in some twenty hours. If she could escape, her survival would depend upon strength and skill she didn't think she possessed.

At nightfall, the wagon jarred to a sudden stop, and the older man released an angry stream of unrecognizable words. He met Harvey at the back of the wagon, and they quietly conferred. She listened and tried to see out the front opening. She scanned the unfamiliar terrain as the men discussed their situation. The older man said something was broken beneath the wagon. Harvey expressed his concern for his brother and said they should wait there for him. His father replied they would only stay for the night, then they would abandon the wagon in the morning and continue to the bridge. He assured Harvey that

Christopher would meet them there, but Harvey repeatedly interjected his belief that some misfortune had befallen his brother.

Mandy sat back against the rough wall inside the wagon. With her finger, she traced a tiny white flower in the print of her yellow summer dress as she thought about what the men were saying. Maybe Everett had been able to fight off Bethany's attacker. Maybe Bethany was safe at home. She prayed that was the case and realized she had no reason to remain with her captors. She decided to find a way to escape. But if an opportunity to sneak off didn't soon arise, she may have to fight for her freedom. Her body ached from her injuries, and a physical altercation would only exacerbate her wounds. She accepted the fact her freedom may cost her life and decided she would rather be dead than forced to be Harvey's mate.

* * *

During the long night camped in the broken-down wagon, Harvey and his father snored as they slept with Mandy wedged between them. She remained awake through the night—her second night without sleep. She tried several times to move out of the wagon, but the men always stirred. By morning, her mind was worn with fatigue and she realized if she didn't escape soon, her day would be spent riding horseback with Harvey to whatever atrocity the men had devised. She couldn't endure another day in captivity, let alone the rest of her life, which she accepted would be short.

As the men prepared to leave the wagon, she recognized her last chance to escape. She used the fear her feminine excuse inflicted on the uneducated men and it provided her the few minutes of privacy she needed to slip away into the woods alone.

Thick clouds filled the eastern sky. She leaned her palm against a tree trunk for balance and glanced up to check the sun's position before the advancing rain clouds obscured it. The pine tree's bark felt rough under her skin.

Agony stabbed through her chest with each inhalation. If she passed a gray leaf tree as she trekked through the unfamiliar forest, she would fill her dress pocket with its leaves and then chew them for their pain-relieving properties. Only hot tea brewed from ground gray leaves would bring her complete healing. But there was no time to think of that now. She moved away from the tree and hoped she would be able to continue east even when the sun was no longer available to confirm her bearings.

As she escaped through the brush, she forced her body to take each step. The terrain was a jumble of boulders, steep grades of embankment, and thick tree roots that jutted from the earth's surface. As she wondered how far back Harvey and his father were, she slipped on some decaying pine needles and tumbled through the ferns into a ravine below. Then she heard Harvey and his father approaching. Though writhing in pain, she tucked her body beneath the cover of a snarled clump that arched from a massive uprooted tree. She listened to their muffled voices coming from the top of the embankment. Harvey wanted to continue searching for her, but his father said she was too much trouble and they would find him a wife elsewhere. She knew which voice belonged to which man and despised the fact she had been with them long enough to discern between the men. If they found her, she would die—if not from the injury that shot pain through her chest then by her own volition. She held still and waited for them to go back to their horses and leave the forest.

She remained hidden long after Harvey and his father went away. When she finally inched out of the dirt, the sky was overcast and the wind blew cooler air across the Land. It took every ounce of strength she had to stand up straight. She pressed her fingers to her breastbone and felt the heat from her swollen flesh. As she trudged through the forest, her stomach growled with incessant hunger pangs.

The thought of her father and mother agonizing over her abduction urged her forward through the woods. It would take days to walk the distance back to Good Springs—if starvation didn't impede her. She stopped when mist from above drew her attention to the clouds. Thick, black puffs billowed furiously overhead, and the fine spray turned into steady rain. As she scanned the woods around her for a place to rest, her foot caught on a tree root. She slipped and landed near the bulbous trunk of an ancient oak. Its ample foliage seemed to block most of the rain, and its old limbs drooped close to the ground, providing an ideal hiding place. She crawled to the tree's base and rested her back against it. She stretched her feet out along the earth. Rain dripped from a leaf and trickled over her ankles. The cool water felt good as it eroded little trenches in the dirt that caked her skin.

Her every breath was met with pain, but it was offset with the joy that she was free. She leaned her head against the rough tree bark and let her eyelids fall shut. She tried to focus on the thought of reuniting with her family, yet each pleasant image she conjured was shattered by the traumatic residue of being held against her will.

Harvey's words echoed in her mind—he had said he took her because she smiled at him. It was true. She had been bored on a hot afternoon and male attention—any male attention—appealed to her. She had tried to arouse interest in him just as she habitually treated every man. The outcome of that indiscretion plunged regret deep into her soul. That impropriety wasn't her first, but she resolved it would be her last. If she lived and made it home to the village, she would keep to herself and her family, denying any desire for attention ever to arise within her again.

Lost in the forest far from home and sheltered beneath the sturdy old tree, she let the weight of fatigue draw her into a deep sleep.

CHAPTER SIX

L evi, Connor, and Everett followed the wagon's tracks until the darkness of night forced them to stop and camp. They resumed their pursuit at daybreak. By afternoon, they spotted the wagon in a clearing. As they drew near, the absence of horses and men filled Levi with anxious concern. Everett pulled back and looked at Levi who, in turn, glanced at Connor, who motioned with his hand to approach the wagon.

Ready to fight, Levi's adrenaline surged; however, the wagon's abandonment meant they had to search the fern-covered forest floor for more tracks. Everett found hoof prints in the dirt that aimed in one direction, but the tracks seemed to circle back and their final direction was elusive. Levi discovered boot prints that led in the opposite direction. With more rain clouds swirling overhead, the three men agreed to spread out and search before any remaining tracks were washed away.

With few discernable tracks to follow, Levi ignored the rain pelting his brow and tied his horse to a tree. He stepped over a log and walked east into the unfamiliar forest. As he trudged around uprooted trees and mossy boulders, he feared the afternoon would slip into evening before he found any more tracks.

He spotted a ravine and decided to continue his search to its edge before he turned back for the night. As he came upon the slope, the rain drove his eyes downward. He noticed grooves in the soil, and the pine needles and sticks were displaced as if someone had recently slid down the embankment. He maneuvered down the steep ridge of earth and leapt over a log at the bottom. He followed the scuffs in the moss of the forest floor until they ended near a substantial oak tree. Its low-lying branches were thick with foliage and hid its base. He squatted to peer beneath the limbs.

* * *

Mandy drew a breath and tried to move, but her muscles didn't respond. The deep sleep that engulfed her body taunted her mind with dreams alternating between wistful and horrific. The bulky folds of the tree trunk she rested against seemed softer now, but she wasn't fully awake and assumed the feeling was part of a dream. The surface against her face didn't feel like rough tree bark, but like warm cloth and— when she listened closely—below the sound of the rain, she heard a steady, repeating thump like the beat of a heart. Her dream of a strong and kind tree with a beating heart and soft bark was the sweetest image to play upon her mind in two and a half days.

Then there was only darkness. The stench of the wagon seeped into her dream. Hard, flat planks of wood were beneath her body. She opened her eyes; it wasn't a dream. She was back in that horrid wagon. It wasn't moving. A hand touched her. She gasped and sat up, sending pain through her chest.

"Shhh, Mandy, it's me. It's Levi."

She heard the voice, the rain, her breath. She was awake. She panted and held still as her heart pounded in her aching chest. Then she reached out to the figure in the dark.

"You're safe, Mandy. I'm here." He took her hand and she felt the calluses on his skin caused by years of carpentry work. She traced her finger along the soft scar on his palm; the skin there felt like silk.

"Levi?" Her voice hurt and it cracked when she said his name.

"Yes, it's me. You're safe now. I found you and brought you here. You're going to be all right."

She wasn't dreaming—he was with her. He had carried her through the forest in the rain. She had been found. As her eyes adjusted to the lack of light, she pulled herself close to Levi and laid her head against his chest. His arms came around her to comfort her, but when he touched her she winced.

"Are you hurt?"

"Yes."

"How badly?"

"I don't know."

"We will get you to Lydia as quickly as we can."

"We?"

"Everett and Connor are here too. We separated to search for you. They'll meet us here soon."

She glanced to the opening at the back of the parked wagon. Rainwater was streaming down from the wagon cover. It was dark outside, but she wanted to see Everett. She thought of the last time she saw him—walking on the road with the men riding into the village behind him. "What happened to Bethany?"

"She's fine. Everett saved her."

"And her attacker? What became of him?"

"He fell under the horse—took a hoof to the skull."

Mandy remembered Harvey's suspicion something had happened to his brother. "Is he dead?"

"Quite." Levi sounded pleased.

"Harvey and his father have gone to meet him at a bridge to the west. When he doesn't show up, they will return to Good Springs." Mandy's relief from being rescued struggled for a grip inside her mind. She curled her fingers into the wet sleeve of Levi's shirt. "They will come back. When they realize he is dead, they will come back for me and for Bethany."

"Not now. Not tonight." Levi's voice was low and sure. "They won't touch you again, Mandy. I promise."

She thought of her parents and wanted to ask, but the threat of weeping closed her throat. She waited for the feeling to pass. When she could tell it wouldn't relent until she knew, she swallowed and whispered, "Are my parents well?"

"No, but they will be. We will get you home as quickly as possible."

The constriction in her throat didn't cease. "My father's heart—"

"He will be very happy to see you." Levi's chin touched the top of her head. "Please, rest now."

He remained still and held her gently. Lying against him, she felt the steady rise and fall of his chest with each breath. The rain sounded lighter on the wagon's cover and the drops became less frequent. Finally, Mandy heard nothing at all.

* * *

The rain stopped before dawn and faint light filtered through the openings in the wagon's cover. Levi had remained awake through the night with his back against the inside wall and Mandy draped across his chest. He had twice tried to move her sleeping body for her comfort during the night, and both times she snapped awake then laid her head back at his chest. There was once a time he would have considered a night holding Mandy to be a dream come true, but he never wanted it to be like this.

In the dim light Levi saw the bruises along her bare arms and understood why she had winced when he touched her. With his finger he lightly moved a curl of hair off her face. His heart broke for her. He regretted every selfish desire he had entertained about her and wanted to kill the men who did this to her. She was broken and he wanted her healed. He could give her the medicine he brought with him, fix the wagon, and take her to Lydia. That was all he could do. It didn't seem like enough.

Everett approached the wagon. "Levi?"

"In here," Levi answered.

Mandy stirred and sat up as Everett looked in the back of the wagon.

"You found her!" Everett climbed into the confined space with them.

Levi slid out of the way and put up his hand. "Be careful, Everett. She's injured."

Mandy touched her fingers to Everett's face. "You came for me."

Levi moved to get out of the wagon and let Everett comfort his sister. The sooner he repaired the wagon, the sooner they could get Mandy home. Connor stood outside the wagon. As Levi put his feet on the ground and began to speak to Connor, he heard Mandy's raw voice behind him.

"Levi—"

He turned and looked at her. Her skin was pale, her eyes were bloodshot, and her dress was stained and rumpled, yet even in her broken state, he found her no less beautiful. "Yes?"

"Thank you."

He nodded in acceptance, and then wondered if her strained voice was the result of screaming. He wasn't prepared for the fear that engulfed him and had to look away before his expression betrayed his worried thoughts.

Connor held the reins of both his horse and Everett's. He motioned with his head for Levi to come with him as he led the horses through the mud. Connor wrapped the reins around a tree branch. "Where did you find her?"

"Under a tree about a mile from here. Where were you and Everett last night?"

"In a cave. We followed some tracks until dark. Everett noticed a cave in the rock, so we went to check it out and ended up waiting out the storm in there—horses and all." Connor gave the horse a pat then turned to Levi. "Is she hurt?"

Levi thought of the bruises across Mandy's skin and the painful sound of her breathing as she slept during the night. "Yes." He stepped to his horse and opened the leather bag strapped to the saddle. Beneath a change of clothes, he felt the jar of gray leaf medicine Lydia had sent with him. "I saw a lot of bruises, but I know there is more to it than that. She can barely speak."

Connor propped his hands on his hips and looked off into the distance. "Listen, Levi—where I come from, people go through things like this all the time. The physical wounds are only half of it. She's going to cry herself to sleep for a long time. She will need her family and Lydia... and you."

Levi held the jar of medicine in his hand and looked at Connor. "I would do anything for her. I mean that—anything. I can fix the wagon and get her home but other than that... what can I do for her?"

"Just stay close. Ask her what she needs... and maybe put the past aside. Consider another perspective on what happened between you and her years ago if you need to. But try to let it go."

"I already have. From the moment I heard she was taken I've regretted being bitter toward her. I no longer hold anything against her. I just want her healed." He started to walk back to the wagon and held up the gray leaf oil. "This should help."

Connor walked beside him and pointed at the wagon. "Let's fix this thing so we can get her to Lydia. We can clean out the back and spread our bedrolls in there for her. Everett can stay back there with her. If we return by the route on Samuel's map, we could shave a few hours off the trip."

Levi nodded. "And once she is safely home, I want to discuss how we will take care of Felix and Harvey. They must pay for this."

* * *

Mandy used the gray leaf tree oil that Levi gave her. She remembered how Lydia applied the formula on Levi's injured hand two weeks prior and she hoped it would bring her quick healing as well. Everett found bruises across her back and carefully rubbed the medicine over her wounds. When he was finished, he told her the oil had made his fingers numb. The medicine's powerful relief quickly seeped through Mandy's skin. The pain deep within her chest decreased but didn't dissipate. She had always heard how the gray leaf medicine removed pain, and though she felt better, she didn't feel any of the euphoric bliss she expected.

Levi and Connor fixed the wagon and readied the horses to leave the mossy forest. Mandy lay on the bedrolls in the back of the cleaned-out wagon, and Everett sat beside her. She slept off and on as they traveled toward Good Springs. After a full day of travel in the repaired wagon, she felt desperate to put her feet on the ground. She sat up and leaned against her brother's shoulder. Levi and Connor were sitting on the front bench driving the wagon. Through the space between them she saw the landscape ahead. It was no longer the dark forest of pine and fern. The recognizable terrain of the gray leaf trees and grass brought Mandy satisfying relief. She noticed a creek ahead and glanced at Everett.

"Do you think they will drive until dusk?"

"Probably. We need to get you to Lydia as soon as possible."

He was right and she knew the men were doing everything they could to help her, but she felt confined in the wagon and was anxious for the jarring motion to stop. The creek came into full view. Then the wagon turned and they were near the water. "I need to stop here."

Everett studied her for a moment, then he nodded and moved to the front opening in the wagon cover. He spoke to Levi and Connor before he scooted back beside her. The wagon rattled to a halt. Everett jumped out the back and took her hand to help her down.

The running creek murmured softly just beyond the trees. It called to her. She yearned to feel the clean, soothing water against her skin. She grabbed Everett's sleeve. "I need to go to the water."

He nodded. "Go ahead. I will be right here."

"No." The thought of being alone frightened Mandy, and her nerves threatened her with a faint quivering sensation. She shook her head. "I can't go alone. You have to come with me."

He held up a finger and stepped over to the front of the wagon as Levi came down from the bench. Mandy turned her back to them and faced the water.

The men whispered for a moment. Then Everett came beside her and they walked together between tall shrubs, gray leaf trees, and the thick undergrowth to get to the water.

Mandy cast her gaze over the flowing creek and looked back to make sure Levi and Connor couldn't see her from where they stood near the wagon. She didn't want their attention nor to elicit their desire. Before the attack she would have secretly hoped men watched her in a moment like this—or at least hoped they would want to watch her even if they were strong enough to control their eyes—but now she loathed the thought and herself for ever being that way. It was that inclination that got her attacked in the first place.

She glanced at her brother. His hair fell over his forehead and he didn't bother to flip it off. His expression held a mix of compassion and concern. "Mandy, what can I do to help you?"

"Stay nearby but don't look at me," she said.

"All right." He moved to the other side of a gray leaf tree and leaned his back against its thick trunk.

She toed off her shoes and looked down at the front of her dress. Only two of the buttons remained. "Say something, so I know you're there."

"What would you have me say?"

"Anything."

There was a long pause and she turned to see if Everett was still there. She saw his back against the tree. Then he spoke. "Did that man violate you?"

"No."

"Don't lie to me, Mandy."

"He did not. Why would you ask that?"

"Because I want to know how slowly I should kill him." His words came with the deep tone of an angry man. He didn't sound like the sanguine younger brother she grew up with on a sheep farm in Good Springs. She realized she wasn't the only person traumatized by the abduction, but she couldn't talk about it.

"Speak of something else."

"I can't think of anything else."

"You must. I need to hear your voice. Tell me a story—from when we were children. Any story. Just speak. Please."

"Fine... one time when you were in the village, Grandfather and I hiked to the springs..."

As Everett spoke, Mandy turned back around and faced the creek. She unbuttoned her dress and let it drop to the ground around her feet. The sun was warm and the thin cotton of her clothes would dry quickly, so she took the dress to the edge of the water and scrubbed it as vigorously as her weak arms allowed. Then she hung the dress from a leafless branch and repeated the process with her underclothes.

The clear water flowed steady and gentle; the creek was full from the previous night's rain. The blue of the empty sky reflected on the creek's rippled surface. The water beckoned her with the promise of cleansing. She stood at the creek's pebbled edge and dipped her toes in the cool and soothing water. The appearance of her feet distorted as a series of small waves passed over them. Each ripple of water climbed higher over her foot and gently stroked her skin. As she stepped farther into the creek, the water rose to her knees then to her waist. Minnows scattered from beneath her feet. The gentle movement of the water conformed to her body as she bent her knees and leaned back; the current was strong enough to keep her upright, but gentle enough to leave her feet on the pebbles below. She treaded the water with her arms, allowing the smooth force of the liquid to cleanse her. Her head rested against the water's surface, relieving her neck from the pull of her waterlogged hair, and in that moment she felt weightless.

She opened her eyes and stared at the sky, longing to float through it, away to some thing—some place of liberty and beauty. Though the water soothed, her healing would come from above. A falcon circled in her view overhead. It used the air's current to soar. She waited for it to flap its wings, but it simply glided around and around in the sky. As she watched the bird, time escaped her and her nerves began to calm.

She could still hear Everett's voice, but the water rippling over her ears disguised his words. She didn't know how long he would speak or even how long she had already been in the water. She only knew she wanted to stay in the middle of the perfect water, untouched and unseen. Though she would have to leave the water, she would do everything she could to remain unnoticed when she returned home. Her past seemed so dissolute, having lived for the entertainment of meaningless attention. She resolved to leave that past in the water with the filth that washed from her flesh, and she stepped back to the shore clean and refreshed.

She walked to her sun-dried clothes grateful for the clear water and warm sunshine. Her dress was ruined but clean. She shook it out and slipped it on, then she bent to pick up her shoes. Something protruding from the pebbles nearby caught her eye. She picked it up then slipped on her shoes and walked back to Everett. She held out the little novelty to her brother. He was mid-sentence, recanting some story involving their grandfather and a jackrabbit. He stopped talking and took the trinket from her palm. "What is it?"

"I don't know. I found it near the creek."

The small device was constructed of hard black material with tiny letters and numbers etched in its surface. Thin colored strands of strange material dangled from one end, each strand encasing metal strings. Mandy didn't have the cognitive energy to be concerned. "Show it to Connor."

Everett nodded and studied the strange device carefully as he walked her back to the wagon.

* * *

Levi lay flat on his back and stared up at the stars. The night was cool enough to warrant a blanket, yet he remained uncovered on top of his bedroll, which was spread over the grass between the back of the wagon and Everett. Everyone else was asleep and silent; occasionally, the horses—tethered to a nearby gray leaf tree—snorted and lifted a hoof.

When they had camped for the night, Connor made a fire and Levi boiled water to make tea from gray tree leaves for Mandy. She had said it helped—

though Levi could tell she was injured worse than she would admit—and she crawled into the back of the wagon where she fell asleep.

Now the embers of the fire had died and the moon had trekked halfway across the sky; its oval shape seemed normal to Levi. Connor always insisted the moon was round and appeared round in the sky from every other viewpoint on earth except here in the Land. But this was the only viewpoint Levi knew and—no matter how often Connor told him to consider other perspectives—the moon, as he saw it, was oval.

Levi heard movement inside the wagon. He wondered if Mandy were awake or simply moving in her sleep as she had the night before in his arms. He listened and waited, in case she needed something.

Her voice came in a broken whisper. "Everett?" She paused and then tried again. "Everett?"

Levi looked at Everett, who was lying on a woolen blanket on the ground between him and Connor. Everett was asleep with one arm over his head and his mouth half open. Levi inhaled and pushed himself to his feet. He stepped to the back of the wagon and leaned his hands against its gate as he peered inside. "What do you need?"

Mandy sat up from where she was lying on the bedroll Connor had brought for her. She tucked her arms beneath the blanket and cleared her throat. "I need Everett."

"He's asleep. Do you want me to wake him?"

"No… I guess not."

The moonlight seeped through the wagon's cover and Levi could see her eyes watching him. He wished he could be like Connor, who seemed always to anticipate the needs of others. Levi felt not only a willingness to help but also desperation to meet her needs. The novel sensation drove him to seek clear direction. "Tell me what you need."

"I can't be alone in here." Her voice was small and childlike—a sharp contrast to the bold and autonomous woman she had been.

He realized she was sleeping in the place that had once been her prison and he understood her fear. "Do you want to sleep out here by your brother?"

"No."

"What can I do?"

"Come in here with me."

Though taught to care about how things might appear to other people, he trusted himself and the men with him. Besides, he had something he needed to say to her and decided this was as good a time as any. He sighed. "Fine. Move over."

"Thank you," she whispered as she scooted to the edge and lay back down.

He climbed into the wagon bed beside her. Reclining on his side with his hand propped under his ear, he looked at her. She was on her back, facing the arched canvas ceiling. He traced the silhouette of her face with his eyes and waited to see if she would go back to sleep or try to talk to him. He knew her well enough to expect the latter.

She turned her head toward him and drew a breath. "Everett said we should be home before noon tomorrow." Her voice was quiet and raspy.

"Yes." When he said no more, she turned her face back to the ceiling and he regretted his reticence.

He wanted to speak and could tell she was still awake, but he waited. Guilt had grated his mind since the moment he heard she had been abducted, and he couldn't bear it any longer. "There is something I need to tell you."

She turned her head toward him but said nothing.

"I want you to know I'm sorry for the way I have treated you."

Her eyebrows rose. "You rescued me, Levi. That's not something you should apologize for."

"No, I mean before that... for years... ever since..." He couldn't bring himself to say it. She wasn't to blame for his reaction to her rejection. "I was bitter toward you. I saw you as nothing more than a beautiful source of pain. I regret my behavior. You and I grew up together, but I allowed my selfishness to diminish our friendship and for that I am sorry."

She was silent. He hoped for a quick reply of acceptance. He even expected an acerbic remark but not silence. He wondered if it was the attack and abduction that had crushed her spirit or if Felix and Harvey had inflicted more harm while they held her captive. He wanted the fiery, provoking Mandy back—he knew how to deal with her. This broken, quiet woman worried him. "Mandy?"

She rolled toward him and reclined on her side, using her arm for a pillow. Then she looked at him. "I will accept your apology to ease your guilt, but I hardly think it's necessary. You offered me love and I taunted you. You weren't the only one—my pleasure came from toying with men's affection, but no more. I hope to live the rest of my life never being desired again. The very thing that once gave me such pleasure, I now find detestable. It's my fault. I got what was coming to me. I have seen the result of my behavior and I'm ashamed."

"You can't possibly believe this was your fault... that what you have been through was some kind of punishment for batting your eyelashes at men. You are innocent." Levi tried to keep his voice down, but his words poured with passion.

"I am not innocent."

"Did he take that from you?"

"Harvey?"

"Yes, Felix's son? Did he steal your innocence?" Levi's anger against Felix and Harvey burned with fervent hatred.

"No. I lost that long ago."

He could barely see her features in the dark. Despite her words he didn't believe she would give herself away knowing what that meant for her future in their village. Someone must have forced her. "Who did that to you?"

Mandy was silent again. He heard her swallow and he waited for her to speak. She looked at his face but not his eyes. "The summer I turned nineteen, the shearers came. One was several years older than me. I felt flattered by his attention and I gave in to his advances—"

"No, Mandy. Don't say it—"

"I must. It is the truth. I did it willingly. The shearer left the village soon after, and I never saw him again. No one knew what I had done... except Lydia. She has kept my secret all these years. I knew no good man would have me after that, but it didn't matter to me then. All I lost was my ability to regret, but somehow… this nightmare has returned that ability to me. Now I regret it and every lascivious thought I've ever had." Her gaze met his. "Now that my secret is out, do you wish to withdraw your apology?"

"No." His answer came quickly and he meant it. Regardless of the village's tradition, he wouldn't reject her—not for that or any other reason.

"I will understand if you choose never to speak to me again." Her voice sounded raw.

Levi wanted to reach out to her but kept his hands where they were. He was drawn more by her vulnerability than he had ever been by her flirting. "I won't hold your past against you and I promise never to speak of it."

"Thank you, Levi." Mandy was still and quiet for a moment. Then she raised herself and pulled a satchel under her head for a pillow. She tugged her blanket close to her chin and then held still again.

Levi watched her face until her eyes slowly closed. He heard her short, shallow breaths. Despite taking the medicine, she was still in pain. He had never known anyone to have pain that tea made from the gray leaf tree didn't immediately remove.

He shifted slightly and she gripped his arm. Her eyes shot open. "Please, don't leave."

"I won't leave you."

She left her hand on his arm but lessened her grip.

Levi remained motionless. He listened to her breathe and thought about her confession—not her words but her tacit need for restoration. Instead of seeking to secure her affection for himself, he wanted to be a part of her healing by confirming her and strengthening her. Connor had said the physical wounds were only half of it, and Levi knew what that meant as he watched her fall back to sleep. Restoration for Mandy wouldn't be a simple return to her previous condition—even she had said she hoped never to elicit desire again. Her restoration would require redemption.

He considered what her secret meant for her as a woman in the Land: a life lived unwed, not out of choice—which held no shame—but out of disgrace. Though no one knew her secret except Lydia and now him, he would keep his promise never to speak of it. He would never shame her.

He took Connor's advice to consider her perspective, and he found little wonder in the fact she had floated through suitors, deflecting every serious attempt for her heart. By tradition, she would have to confess her ruined virtue to accept any proposal, and rare would be the man willing to dishonor himself by taking a wife who was by tradition considered marred. To protect herself and her family she had carefully guarded her heart. He wanted that to be his duty.

As he studied her delicate fingers still touching his arm, he realized she had never been loved for who she was—faults and all—not by him or any other man. Her hope was now to remain undesired and, if that were what she needed, he would put aside his attraction to her. She needed protection, both physically and for her dignity—and he could provide that. His presence and comfort may help her heal and lead to her restoration, but for some reason it still didn't seem like enough.

CHAPTER SEVEN

Levi opened the back door of the Fosters' farmhouse and held it as Everett walked Mandy inside. Roseanna gasped with startled delight and dropped a jar of pickled beets on the kitchen floor. She rushed past the puddle of purple juice, soggy roots, and broken glass to get to her daughter. Levi took care of the mess while Roseanna wept joyfully over Mandy's return. As Roseanna escorted Mandy to her bedroom, Everett ran to the barn to tell Samuel the good news, and Connor took the wagon to get Lydia.

Levi listened to the muffled sounds of Mandy and Roseanna's tearful reunion as he scooped the glass and beets from the kitchen floor with a tea towel. He dropped the sticky mess into the rubbish bin then looked up as the back door banged open and Samuel dashed by. Everett walked in the house after his father and coolly closed the door. Its latch made a sharp click against the strike plate. Everett went to the kitchen sink and filled a glass with water. Then he sat at the table and put his feet on the chair across from him. He looked pleased with himself, and his pride was well deserved.

Levi wiped the floor and rinsed the beet juice from his fingertips. He dried his hands on his trousers as he stepped to the table and pulled out a chair. As he sat, Lydia burst through the Fosters' front door. She held her medical bag and panted as she glanced at Levi. He rose and pointed to the hallway. She disappeared into the corridor without saying a word.

Connor, John, and Bethany hurried into the house after Lydia. Levi met them near the front door. Bethany clasped her arms around him then let go and moved directly to Everett in the kitchen. Levi watched as Everett stood and embraced her. Their friendship appeared to be intimate but if there were more, it remained unsaid. After witnessing Everett's behavior—searching and caring for Mandy—Levi would gladly bless a union between Everett and Bethany.

John put his hand on Levi's shoulder. "I am proud of you, son. Connor gave me the details on the way here." Levi nodded at his father.

Samuel stepped out of Mandy's bedroom. Silence blanketed the room as he came from the hallway. He raised both palms. "Doctor Bradshaw sent me out of the room—she said she can't hear Mandy's heartbeat with me blubbering." Samuel gave a small smile; his eyes were happy but red from crying. He stuck out his hand to Levi. "I can't thank you enough. She told us how you found her." He shook Levi's hand then yanked him into a hug and patted his back heartily.

When Samuel released Levi, he reached for Connor. "You brought my daughter home. Thank you!" He turned to the kitchen table. "And Everett! You have proven yourself valiant, son." Samuel continued his jovial commendations as he walked to the kitchen.

The men followed Samuel and he gestured for them to sit at the table. Bethany removed herself from the kitchen and went into Mandy's bedroom with the other women. Connor sat beside Levi at the table. He leaned back in the wooden chair and pulled something out of his trouser pocket. Levi looked at the small, black device as Connor picked at its colored wires. Levi nudged Connor. "What is that?"

Connor glanced at Levi then at the other men. He laid the device on the table. "It's part of an electrical wiring harness. Mandy found it by the creek when we stopped yesterday."

Levi stared at the strange clump of wires and plastic. "An electrical wiring harness? How did it get to the Land?"

"It's probably debris from the aircraft." Connor shifted sideways in his chair and put his arm over the back of it, effusing nonchalance.

Samuel shrugged and returned to the subject at hand. "John, there are locks on every house in the village. People are not allowing their children to play out-of-doors."

John nodded. "I know. I have kept Bethany within my sight for five days. She is anxious to get back to work at the pottery yard." John glanced at Connor. "And I have kept watch over Lydia, too, of course. Despite what happened, they have already grown weary of my safeguarding."

Samuel lowered his voice. "Roseanna stands and looks out the window for several minutes before she walks to the garden. I know a lot of that had to do with Mandy being gone, but she is still truly afraid they will come back and cause more destruction."

"We can't live in fear forever," John added.

"Felix and Harvey will come back to the village." Everett spoke up, drawing the men's attention for the first time. "It's simply a matter of when."

"It may be years." Samuel raised his palm. "It's been eleven years since their last attack in Good Springs."

"Yes, but there is something here that they want." Levi felt his pulse quicken as he thought of them trying to take Mandy or Bethany again. "Mandy said they were planning to meet Christopher at the bridge to the west. When he doesn't show up, they will come back to Good Springs."

Connor's eyes were on the electrical device, his face full of concern. "We need to be prepared when they come."

John crossed his arms over his chest. "Bethany is terrified, and I assume Mandy even more so, but they won't stay locked away indefinitely. I have raised four girls—they will only tolerate the constant guarding for so long."

Levi felt his father's focus was on the wrong aspect of the situation. He leaned forward, resting an arm on the table. "I'm not concerned with whether or not the women find our protection annoying. Felix will come back here—and when he does we need to be ready to fight. He and Harvey must be punished."

John put both hands up. "Levi." He dragged out the word as if warning a small child of possible infraction. "We must try to resolve any confrontation peacefully—"

Levi thought of how his father stood motionless when Felix killed his mother years before. Anger welled within Levi's throat. He slammed his fist onto the table. "No! You can't silence me, Father. I won't stand by while Felix destroys the people I love like you did when he attacked Mother."

The room fell silent. Levi glowered at his father; his stomach felt sour with the bitterness he had held since his mother's death. John didn't speak, nor did he look away. Samuel made some noise and a gesture in an attempt to diffuse the tension, but Levi kept his focus on John.

In one movement John put his elbows on the table and wiped his face with both hands. Connor stood and tapped Everett on the back. Everett followed him to the back door. Samuel met them on the porch. They closed the door, but Levi could still hear their muffled voices.

John exhaled slowly and folded his hands in front of him. He leveled his chin as he peered at Levi. "I know you blame me for your mother's death, son. You may not want my perspective, but you are going to hear it: I had four daughters to protect and Felix Colburn demanded two of them—some nonsense about being a Colburn descendant and his sons deserving Colburn women as wives. Nothing like that had ever happened in the village. I was a man of forty-two years and had never encountered violence. When I denied Felix his demand, he moved quickly and forcefully. He pushed your mother and took off before I knew what had happened. Though I immediately went to her, it didn't occur to me that she would die. You may despise me for the rest of your life if you so desire, but you will never loathe that day more than I do." He leaned back in his chair and narrowed his eyes. "If you need my apology for your mother's death, then I offer it. However, I am the overseer of this village, and if you choose to take issue with me again, you would be wise to do it privately."

Levi looked away from his father. An apology followed by a forceful admonition hardly seemed sincere. He thought of Connor's advice to contemplate different perspectives and decided he would grant his father's words consideration, but now wasn't the time.

John waved the other men back inside, obviously able to see someone's waiting eyes through the windowpane in the door. Connor put his hand on Levi's shoulder before he sat back down.

Levi listened as John told them to keep the women under guard and their doors locked until he met with the village elders. He said they would discuss the situation and—if Felix returned—find a way to resolve it as peacefully as possible. John looked at Levi when he said it and deepened his voice as if to stress his authority, but Levi looked away. His mind was made up—if he encountered Felix or Harvey again, he would administer justice without calling a meeting of the elders or asking for his father's opinion.

Roseanna walked into the kitchen and Bethany followed. The men became silent as Roseanna strode to the sink. She filled a kettle with water and plunked it on the stove with a clank. Lydia stepped into the kitchen from the hallway. Connor stood quickly and his chair made a rumble as it moved across the wooden floor behind him. Levi watched Lydia's face as everyone looked to her for her prognosis. Connor moved close beside her.

Lydia tucked a strand of hair behind her ear. "Mandy has suffered a mild sternal fracture. That isn't an easy bone to break, so I know her body endured severe force. I examined her heart and lungs and, at present, I don't detect any apparent damage." She motioned with her hand at Roseanna, who was working in the kitchen. "We will give her a second dose of gray leaf tea, and I'm ordering bed rest for seven days."

Levi didn't know exactly what the diagnosis implied, but he knew by Lydia's expression it was serious. He wanted to see Mandy before he left, but the flurry of attention she received from her parents and Lydia made his presence feel superfluous. He decided to stay out of the way and walked out to the front porch.

Shep moved from his place on the steps. The dog's tongue lolled to the side as it leaned against Levi's thigh. He gave the dog a pat on the head then descended the steps and walked across the road to his property. Stuffing his hands into his pockets, he looked at his half-built house. With its exterior walls and roof finished, it appeared to be complete, but the inside still needed much work.

* * *

Justin Mercer sat at the lobby bar in the one-time Falkland Island tourist lodge and waited for the South African who went by the name of Volt. The first part of Volt's plan had worked: the computer codes he gave Mercer had successfully sabotaged the icebreaker's engine readings. It bought them the time needed to put together a crew and wait for the island's imminent evacuation. Volt's plan provided the best chance of getting to the coordinates of the uncharted land, and Mercer was beginning to trust him.

As Mercer waited at the bar, his eyes darted—to the front door, the hallway, the lodge's office—after every extraneous sound. Being part of a criminal scheme made him nervous, no matter how much he believed it was essential for his survival. Volt had reassured him no one would be left to care about a missing ship before much longer.

The British Forces' plan to use the icebreaker was public knowledge in the Falklands and made it a challenge for Mercer to furtively find able seaman willing to steal the nuclear-powered ship. The task became even more challenging as illness spread throughout the barracks and lodges. Most of the remaining population in the remote port town consisted of Royal Navy crewmen suffering from a mutated strain of tuberculosis. Inviting a known renegade like Volt to his military-controlled living quarters worried him, but the thought of venturing into a town where most of the people were dying of a communicable disease terrified him even more. If it weren't for that disgusting illness, he would spend his every evening at the bars in town. He missed socializing, and he especially missed women. He needed a drink and rapped his knuckles on the bar's black enamel surface. A glance in the cracked mirror behind the bar confirmed he also needed a haircut. He ran his fingers through his hair a few times then watched the lodge keeper step out of his office.

The lodge keeper wore ladies' glasses, walked with a limp, and was about ninety-six years old in Mercer's estimation. The old man pointed his arthritic finger as he lumbered behind the bar. "What have you got to trade?"

Mercer glanced at the empty shelves behind the bar and back at the old man. "What have you got to drink?"

"Home spirits. I'll pour two fingers worth in exchange for your wristwatch."

"Forget it." He looked away and the old man hobbled back into his office.

Mercer turned on his barstool to face the glass front doors. The lodge keeper had the building locked down even though it was broad daylight. The old man would have to let Volt into the lodge and would probably ask too many questions.

Soon the spiky-haired man with tattoo-sleeves walked up to the door and pressed the buzzer. The old man in the office didn't let him in. As Volt shook the locked lodge door, the old man raised his voice. "Is that bloke here for you?"

"Yes, sir." Mercer grinned, ready to give the old man a diversion. "He's delivering my vitamin order."

"Vitamins, ha!" The old man choked on his laughter. "Nobody has vitamins. He's a dope dealer is what he is. I knew it the moment I saw him."

Mercer stood and hid both hands in his pockets. "Yes, sir. You've figured me out. He's my dealer. Now let him in or I'll die from withdrawal."

The old man murmured something about punk drug addicts, and then the front door buzzed. The click of the lock inside the door echoed in the small lobby, and Volt pulled the door open. He stepped into the lodge and wiped his sandaled feet on the hibiscus-print welcome mat then walked toward Mercer. Volt smiled as if it were a social engagement. It would have perturbed Mercer, but he had learned Volt was genuinely friendly—an attribute that came in stark contrast to his life work of causing great ruin for the highest bidder.

As Mercer started walking to the tiled hallway that led to his room, he motioned with his finger for Volt to keep silent. Volt nodded and walked a pace behind. Once in his room, Mercer closed and locked the door then turned to Volt. "You can't speak in front of the old man. I don't trust him."

"What I have to say is no secret: the cruise ship is almost here. I heard it over the radio this morning." Volt played with the small patch of whiskers below his bottom lip as he spoke. "People are packing their bags and coughing their way to the pier."

"It's about time." Mercer walked to the window and put his hand to the blinds. He spread his fingers and widened the space between the plastic slats to get a clearer view of the pier. "The officers are anxious to get to Valparaiso. They won't do a thorough evacuation."

"People in town are saying anyone who doesn't make it to the dock will be left behind to die."

Mercer let go of the blinds and brushed his hands together as he turned to Volt. "You should stay away from the people in town before you catch it, too."

"Don't worry about me, mate." Volt sat in the wicker chair and crossed his legs at the ankle. "I never get sick."

Mercer thought of the few civilians still on the island, now ill and soon to be stranded without medication. He rarely entertained humanitarian concerns because it immediately turned his thoughts to his parents and brother. He had lost contact with his family during the initial stages of the world war and assumed they were dead. He had found the grief distracting while in the cockpit until he trained himself not to think of them. Once he disciplined himself to put aside the thought of the dead and dying, he learned to focus on his survival. Now his work was securing a ship to get to the uncharted land before he lost the chance, and he intended to keep his focus under control. He walked to the unmade bed and sat on the edge of the mattress. "I know you get more information than just what comes over the radio. What's really going on out there?"

"With the rest of the world, you mean?" Volt uncrossed his ankles and began to bounce one leg at the knee with rapid, anxious movements. "The Arab communication reports estimate ninety percent of Earth's pre-war population is gone. The Chinese claim victory over Russia. The Russians claim victory over China."

"What about the States? Anything from the States?"

"No, mate. Communications aren't getting through." Volt seemed to realize his work had affected Mercer's people and his tone changed. "But Americans don't need satellite communications to survive. You Yanks find a way to get back on top—refuse defeat, never surrender, vow to rebuild and all that. The important thing is you have a new land to search for. It looks like we will be on our way any day now."

"Yeah," Mercer mumbled. "Any day now."

Volt picked at the loose strings hanging from the torn fabric on the knee of his jeans. "We will probably rock up to that land and surprise the blazes out of your aviator friend. He's been there, what, two years now? He's probably made himself a grass skirt and has a coconut for a girlfriend."

The imagery made Mercer chuckle. "Maybe."

"What'll you name the place—Mercerland?"

Mercer's gaze became fixed on the strings hanging from Volt's jeans, but his vision blurred as if his brain had briefly lost function. Maybe Lieutenant Bradshaw was the only person on that landmass, or maybe a whole civilization already lived there. Maybe there were women in grass skirts. He wouldn't know until he got there, but he hoped there would be women.

Volt continued his glib chatter. "Name it after yourself, mate, after all you've done to find it. I won't mind a bit. As long as I can build a hut with an ocean view and there's no more talk of a world war—that's all I want." Volt rolled a piece of the bluish-white string and dropped it to the floor. "So what's he like?"

Mercer watched the string fall to the floor. "Hm?"

"The aviator—what's his name?"

"Lieutenant Bradshaw—Connor Bradshaw."

"What was he like?"

"Connor was an excellent aviator. He was smart and controlled. We flew several missions together in the weeks before the crash. He was a year ahead of me at the academy, so I knew of him before I was assigned to his squadron. He was a good guy too— had a lot of friends, liked to play cards, got along with everyone, but he never drank or slept around. He was the type who was at the gym early and at the library late." Mercer was shocked by his own words. He looked Volt in the eye. "I'm talking about him like he's dead. He isn't. I watched his parachute drift toward the land. I know he's there, alive."

Volt nodded and shifted in his seat. "Yeah, mate. He's there and he sounds like a cool bloke. I can't wait to meet him."

It surprised Mercer how easy it was for Volt to get him to talk. It had been two years since he had met anyone he considered a friend, and he never thought he would be comfortable around a man like Volt. Mercer cleared his throat. "Have you secured any of the crew yet?"

"I've got eight men who are definitely in." He counted on his fingers as he named off positions. "I've got two marine engineers, an electrical engineer, a guy who was a chief mate on a merchant ship for thirty years before the war, and a couple of other crewmen."

"Eight? I thought you said the skeleton crew on that ship was twelve. We could leave any day now, and we need a minimum of four more men."

Volt pointed at himself then Mercer. "The two of us can handle most of the bridge operations."

"I don't want to get five miles out of port and lose power. There's a lot about this ship I don't know."

Volt went back to picking at the strings on his jeans. "I've made off with older, bigger ships on my own. This will be a picnic compared to most of the jobs I've pulled off, believe me. With the computerized propulsion control system and the self-maintaining fresh water generators in that ship, it practically runs itself." He stood to leave. "I'll keep a look out for a couple more men, but the ten of us can handle it just fine on our own. Believe me, mate, this will be like taking a luxury cruise."

CHAPTER EIGHT

L evi wiped the raindrops from his forehead with his sleeve as he stepped inside the Foster house. Roseanna closed the door behind him and giggled when droplets from his wet hair misted her cheek. He chuckled at her as he took off his overcoat and hung it on a brass hook on the wall. Then he pointed at the hallway. "Is it all right if I go into her room?"

"Of course." She gave him a wink then stepped toward the kitchen. "I'm making your favorite tonight, Levi. Mutton!"

"Thank you, Mrs. Foster." He walked down the hallway and knocked lightly on the frame of Mandy's open bedroom door.

"Come in." She smiled and sat up in bed. A red curl dropped in front of her eye as she leaned against the headboard. "I hoped you would visit me this week."

Levi grinned, happy to hear she wanted his company. He pushed his damp hair away from his forehead and stepped inside. Her bedroom was girly with pink ruffled lace around the edges of the quilts and the curtains. He had not been in there in years, possibly not since childhood, and then it was only momentarily as Everett's guest. When they were children, she used to scold any boys who got near her room, and it pleased him that she now invited him in. The feminine room held an arcane quality and Levi felt suddenly privy to some mystery of the opposite sex by being welcome there.

He slid his hands into his pockets and studied her. The color of her skin had improved—though she was naturally pale enough that most people wouldn't notice, Levi did. Red curls sprang from the crown of her head. Each ringlet made a distinct trail until it disappeared behind her back. A few strands framed her face and fell in front of her shoulders. Her eyes were wide and clear. She looked like her old self but without the sultry pretense.

He stepped closer. "How are you feeling?"

"Much better, thank you."

"Lydia said she's confident you will fully recover."

"Yes."

"I'm pleased to hear it."

She gave a slight smile then looked toward the hallway and back at Levi. "Are you staying for dinner?"

He nodded. "I'll be here awhile. Your father asked me to come. The elders are gathering this evening, and Everett has work to do in the barn."

"Ah." She frowned and adjusted the pillow behind her back. "So you're here as my protector?"

"Yes." Levi searched her face. She sounded disappointed, though he didn't understand why. She had at first seemed happy to have him there, so the change in her demeanor confused him. He turned and walked to her window, then he peeled back the frilly curtain. Rain splattered the glass and ran down in quick, jagged streams. He saw the thick patch of forest between the Fosters' front yard and the road. The same amount of vegetation stood between the road and his house. The Fosters' house wasn't visible from his, but still he wondered if he might see his house from her window. He strained his eyes looking for it.

"You don't have to stand guard, you know." Her voice lacked its regular fullness and gave away her incomplete healing.

"I promised your father I would." He turned to face her. "Would you like me to leave your room?"

"No." She smiled again. "You appeared to be taking my father's command to stand guard literally. I meant that you may sit down if you like."

He picked up an armless side chair that was against the wall near the window and carried it close to her bed. He sat and mindlessly brushed lint from his pant leg. It was hard to figure out what she wanted. He laced his fingers together in front of him then looked at her but didn't know what to say. "Can I get you anything?"

"My workbench." She grinned at her own joke.

"I would, but if Lydia found out you were up and working, I would be in trouble."

"Right, well, let's not vex the good doctor." She still smiled, but her joyful expression froze for a moment. She touched her sternum with her fingertips and took a deep breath.

"Are you still in pain?"

She dropped her hand and seemed embarrassed to have drawn attention to her injury. "No. Not really." Her eyes cast downward to her hands on her blanket. He realized she wasn't looking at anything in particular, but some dark thought had claimed her attention internally.

"Mandy?" Her seriousness drew him. She was still broken and he wanted to fix her but didn't know how. He leaned forward, propping his elbows on his knees. "You will heal from this."

She nodded in agreement, but her gaze didn't meet his. Her silence emanated a sense of despair, and his heart mourned with her. He wanted to heal the hurt for her, if only he knew how. He would have taken it on himself if it were possible.

She slid down beneath the blankets. Her hair fanned out over the pillow. Then she lay under the covers, motionless. "What did people say at church yesterday?" Her quiet voice sounded glassy.

He watched her pull the covers up over her chin, concealing most of her face. The room was warm; she wasn't burrowing for heat but for security. "They were concerned for you... and for Bethany. The people who hadn't heard about your return were glad to hear the news." He thought about the Sunday service and the palpable air of tragedy that had prevailed, but he couldn't tell her. "I think everyone will be relieved to see you next week."

"Did they ask the details of what happened to me?"

"Some did."

"What were they told?"

"Only that you and Bethany were attacked, and you were taken by force but later escaped and we brought you home."

"People will want to know more. They will ask the same question you and Everett asked." She was concerned an abundance of questions would expose her past. Her reputation was at stake and—knowing her secret—he understood her fear.

He reached out and pulled the edge of the blanket back so he could see her face. She looked at him, impassive. He wondered what depths he had missed by spending years distracted by her surface. "You don't owe anyone an explanation." He watched her eyes, wanting acknowledgment she understood him. "People are concerned about you. They need to see that you are well, but you don't have to tell them anything. I certainly won't."

Tears pooled in the corners of her eyes then broke free and rolled down her cheeks. She immediately reached up with the edge of the bedsheet and wiped them away. "I'm sorry for crying."

"Don't be."

"No, I am. I'm tired of crying and I should be able to stop it."

"Your tears are beautiful. Let them come."

Her hand halted its dabbing. "I thought men were repelled by crying women?"

He grinned. "Remember, I grew up with four sisters."

"Yes, you have encountered plenty of crying then."

"And it was usually over nothing." He shook his head at the thought. "But it gave me plenty of practice discerning when tears mean something."

She looked down. "It means I'm weak."

"It means you're alive. You're home and safe. If you hadn't made it home, we would all be crying. I assure you, no one is offended by your tears, especially me."

Mandy held a hand out from beneath the blanket and Levi took it. Her small gesture wasn't a coy desire for touch, but simply a friend's request for comfort. He watched her face as she looked at his hand and they sat together, quiet and connected. Her hand felt small in his. She had always seemed strong, but it was a self-assurance only fueled by the constant validation her beauty afforded. Though her outward loveliness had in no way diminished, he found her transparency far more powerful.

His thumb skimmed over her delicate fingers and he thought of the moment when he lifted her broken body from beneath the rain soaked tree. He would give her whatever she needed—and now she needed his comfort and protection. Though she may not want anything else from him, he had never loved her more. He recognized the process from his experience with tragedy and understood this time together—quiet and allowing tears—was reserved for those whom she trusted most.

Her eyes cleared. She looked up at him and tugged his hand an inch closer. "How long did it take?"

"Hm?"

"After they attacked your family... and your mother died..." She looked at his hand then back at his face. "How long did it take until you felt safe again?"

Speaking of her pain didn't bother him, but he wasn't prepared to speak of his own. He shifted in the chair but made sure not to pull his hand away. "That's probably a better question for my sisters. I think girls are affected differently from boys."

Her eyes widened a degree. "Did my question offend you?"

"No." He thought of her question again. "I don't remember feeling unsafe after the attack, only angry. I was twelve years old—too young to lose a mother, but old enough to know what should've happened. And I wasn't injured—physically—as you were."

"It must have been painful nonetheless." Her finely arched brows pulled together and she looked like she was deep in thought. "I just want to know how long this nightmare will last."

"I can't answer that, Mandy. I'm sorry—I wish I could. I want you to feel safe. More than that, I want to keep you safe. But as long as Felix and Harvey are alive, you just have to trust we are doing everything we can to protect you. I'm here and you are safe now."

The unreadable expression returned to her face and she stared at their hands. Relieved her questions about his experience appeared to be over, he relaxed again. He watched her eyes as she gazed at their joined hands. Even if there was nothing more between them, he was honored to have her trust.

After a moment, her lips curved at some thought and she looked up at him. "Do you remember when we were children and my tabby cat had kittens... and Lydia took the little orange one home?"

He instantly recalled his least favorite of Lydia's many childhood pets. He raised an eyebrow. "I hated that cat."

"I believe the feeling was mutual." Mandy grinned and the light hit her eyes.

He nodded. "It would jump on my shoulders when I walked into the barn and scare me to death." He remembered the cat's needle-sharp claws. "And it only felt the need to attack me—never Father or the girls."

"Lydia and I were so amused by that." Mandy turned his hand over while she spoke. He held it open and watched her. With one finger she traced the scar on his palm. Her thin finger wasn't as wide as the thick scar. "Then one day that poor cat went missing." She looked him in the eye.

"I have no idea what happened to that cat."

"Truly?"

"Truly." Levi gave a deadpan expression that matched his tone, but all he could think of was the sensation of her touch along the scar.

Roseanna walked into the room, snapping his attention away from Mandy. "Dinner is ready," she announced as she glanced at their joined hands. Levi let go and Roseanna smiled as she walked back to the kitchen, humming.

* * *

After completing the prescribed weeklong bed rest, Mandy was anxious to get out of the house. But with the looming possibility of her attackers returning, her father had ordered her to go no farther than the barn. He agreed if she locked the door—and went to and from the barn only with an escort—she could spend her days in her workshop without guard. And so for four straight weeks, Mandy spent every day alone in her workshop.

The days began to blur from one into another. The weather was the same every day: warm but not stifling. Somehow she looked away from her tools and the wood and glanced out the window at the same time every day. The clouds seemed to take the same shapes every day, making her believe the clouds that passed the day before were passing by again. She often forgot the day of the week and what she had eaten for breakfast.

Mandy walked into her workshop determined this day would be different. "It's Tuesday," she said aloud as she slid the bolt of the lock just as Levi had taught her when he installed it weeks before. After setting her dinner pail on a shelf near the door, she looped her hair in a tight swirl behind her head and impaled the bun with the piece of sharpened dowel she kept on her workbench.

A generous flow of creative energy fueled her efforts throughout the day. Time escaped her notice—save for a swath of sunlight near the window that moved across the floor as the day elapsed. After carving out the front piece of a violin body, she gouged and shaped the wood, continually checking its grain and tone. Late in the afternoon, she completed the center strip and the back of the instrument body. Then she took the pieces to the loft window and laid them on the wide ledge to dry. The sun was low and the wood required more time in the sunlight before she would work with it again, so she took a dustpan and straw hand broom and cleaned the scattered chips and shavings from the surface of her workbench.

Dusk changed the light in the workshop and the crickets began their song. Before the attack, a hollow lonely feeling would overtake her as soon as the sun set. But now her emptiness had neither a distinct daily beginning nor a sure fix. Her fear was now so constant it had become a companion in itself, yet her boredom had driven her away from her family's home and out to her workshop. She wished she could walk into the village, not for intrigue but for companionship. The desire to forgo the shame of having her secret exposed kept her resigned to a life alone. She couldn't sit in the house all day, nor walk to the village alone, nor marry and have a family of her own. It was work or sleep—but always alone.

The fading light now simply meant it was time to clean up and wait for her brother or father to come up to the loft and knock on her door. One of them would walk her to the house as they did every night. If it was her father, he would nervously shift his eyes from side to side, in fear Felix or Harvey might appear as he hurried his daughter to the house; if it was her brother, he would strut—not with pride but with fury—in hope the attackers would return on his watch so he could unleash his revenge on them.

She sighed at the thought and turned to clap the full dustpan out the window. The wood shavings swirled and floated on the wind as they scattered across the pasture below. The freshly carved instrument pieces on the window ledge caught her eye. They made her think of the empty space she intentionally created for the inside of each instrument. The shaping of the wood created resonance and determined the instrument's timbre. No matter how beautiful the surface, without emptiness there would be no quality to the instrument's tone. It made her want to play a song. She walked through her workshop and opened the cracked leather case of her favorite violin. A family heirloom, it was the only surviving instrument brought to the Land by the founders seven generations before her. The old violin didn't possess the clarity and brilliance of the new wood instruments, but it was the sound of her musical heritage.

She plucked each string and adjusted the tuning, then she set the violin beneath her chin and raised the bow. Her fingers danced effortlessly on the fingerboard as she drew the bow across the strings. The notes flowed freely from the darkness of the instrument's hollow body; as she thought of the empty space inside the violin, she felt the music resonate in the cavern of her heart.

She closed her eyes and listened to the notes pouring from the sound holes, which were cut precisely to ensure the right volume of air was retained in the instrument to create the resonance. There was an aching hollow inside her heart too, and her past efforts to fill it had left no room for resonance. Maybe that was the purpose of her emptiness: resonance—but not quality of sound but quality of spirit.

She let the last note ring out. Levi had been right—she was healing. But there was more to her heartache than the nightmare she had gone through. The healing she needed wouldn't simply close the wound but would shape her to pour out the life she was created for.

Mandy returned the instrument to its case and carefully latched it closed. She thought of her grandfather every time she played the old instrument. When the antique violin had cracked and needed repairs, her grandfather had been determined to build her a new one. Together they had spent every afternoon for an entire winter in his woodshop dissecting the decrepit instrument and replicating its parts. They made a new violin, but it lacked timbre. Though she cherished the old violin out of sentiment, she had tried again and again to make a violin with a sound close to the heirloom instrument. Finally—mere days after her grandfather's death—she had discovered the unparalleled sound of the gray leaf tree's wood.

In keeping with the tradition of the Land, her grandfather had written notes of his instrument repair procedures in the same way all knowledge was printed and preserved for future generations. Mandy realized that even though her new wood instruments were celebrated throughout the Land, she had yet to document her work as a luthier. With a fresh sense of mortality, she decided it was time to detail the secrets of her instrument making.

She walked to a shelf and pulled out a dust-covered stack of paper, then she carried it to her workbench. Resigned to the notion that she wouldn't have children of her own, she began drafting instructions for whomever would one day take interest in her craft. She started by sketching the shape of the individually carved pieces and began to make notes of dimension and wood treatment and a special note detailing the purpose of emptiness.

"Mandy?" Everett knocked twice when he called her name from the other side of the door. She grinned at the familiar voice and laid her pencil on the paper. She went to the door and slid the lock out of the frame.

Her brother's hair was greased back with a day's worth of sweat, and he smelled like the fields. She appreciated that he spent his days happily working the farm he would one day inherit and understood his love for the animals was comparable to her love for the instruments. Still, she crinkled her nose at him as she stepped back to the workbench to gather her papers.

Everett reached an arm around her and plucked the top paper from her hand. "Nice sketch. You're a bit young to journal your life's work, aren't you?"

"Age has little to do with it. Lydia writes every detail of her work, and she often suggests I begin documenting mine." Mandy snatched the paper and for a moment felt like she and her brother were children again. "Shouldn't you be writing about sheep breeding and whatnot?" She smiled but Everett didn't smile back.

He leaned a palm on the corner of the workbench and hovered over her. He stared at the sketch for a moment and spoke with a low voice. "You thought you were going to die, didn't you?"

"Why would you ask that?" She noticed his serious demeanor and realized she had misjudged her brother's playfulness. She glanced through the window at the pasture beyond as she remembered the attack. "Yes... I did... I still do."

"Is that why you are writing this?" He motioned to the pages. "Do you think they will come back and kill you?"

"We will all die one day—some sooner than others." She pointed to the lock on her workshop door. "I believe you all have made it clear that my day is probably soon."

"It's possible Felix and Harvey will come back, but we are determined to protect you." Everett sighed and put his hand on her shoulder. "I want you to feel safe."

"Levi said the same thing. You all want me to feel safe but to live like I am in danger." She turned to the workbench and gathered the papers. After tapping them to straighten the stack, she looked up at him. The changes in his maturity and manner left nothing of the little brother she knew from childhood. His set jaw was covered in dark stubble; the whiskers diminished his last traces of youth and added to his new ferocity. Through the ordeal, Everett had earned her respect and her dependence. "I appreciate your effort, but this constant guarding doesn't make me feel safe—it just reminds me of the horror I lived through and the possibility it may occur again. And yet, despite what happened, I want to carry on. I just don't know how. I spend my days achingly alone and yet when you all hover about to guard me, I feel as trapped as I did in that wagon. I have been home for over a month. My body has healed but—in my mind—it's not over. I'm still trapped and it's only because of these restrictions. I just want this to end. It's not natural for me to be fearful, and I hate it. And I know it won't end until I can walk outside my door without a guard. If you all won't let me move on, I will have to do it myself."

Everett's brow creased in the center. "It may not be normal for you to live in fear, but since the danger is real, the fear is necessary—it will help us keep you safe. As far as what you endured—you can't skip the healing process just because you're a strong-willed person. The medicine from the gray leaf tree may speed an injury's healing, but you were injured in a deeper sense. You can't rush that kind of healing."

"I don't feel like I'm rushing anything. I don't like to dwell on painful things. I like to get over them. I know parts of this will always be with me and there were parts of me that needed to change, but I understand those things now and I'm ready to heal and move on. I just don't know how I'll live if I'm not even allowed to go outside on my own."

Everett stepped to the door. His expression lightened and he raised a finger. "Then perhaps you need to linger in the healing process but don't dwell on the hurt. That—I'm told—will only lead to bitterness. But you must submit to our protection."

Exasperated, she chuckled at her brother. "You no longer talk like a nineteen-year-old. How did you become so wise?"

"I spent nineteen years listening to you."

"Flattering words, but I hardly agree."

Everett smirked and instantly seemed young again. He opened the door. "Very well then—how would you advise me if I were hurt and the possibility remained that I could be hurt again, but I wanted to—needed to—carry on?"

Mandy stood at the threshold of the door to her workshop and thought of the hollow feeling inside her heart and the resonant space inside her instruments. "I suppose I would tell you to linger in the healing process but don't dwell on the hurt." She smiled at Everett then stepped out the door. "But I can't promise I'll remain under lock and guard much longer."

CHAPTER NINE

L evi turned a handle, decreasing the shower's flow until it stopped dripping. He stepped over the tub's edge and toweled off. As he dressed, he looked back at the perforated metal spout above the bathtub in his nearly completed home. Connor had been right—the controlled release of water from an elevated rain tank made an excellent alternative to filling a bathtub, though it would be far less pleasant in winter unless Levi lit a fire beneath the tank outside. He began to contemplate the idea of heating the tank and imagined what he could build to make that possible.

The silence of his empty house was broken by the muffled sound of voices outside—then a knock at his door. He wiped the towel over his wet face as he left the bathroom and walked to the front door.

Everett was standing with his toes at the threshold, grinning. "Would you like company while you work in your house today?"

Levi saw movement at the bottom of the porch steps and tilted his head to look past Everett. Mandy was standing by the bottom step with her arms crossed firmly in front of her. She wore a pale blue dress that made the color of her hair look like fire.

"Father and I have to ride out to the western pastures today, and Mandy has grown weary of remaining locked away." Everett glanced at his sister then looked back at Levi. "Her wandering from the house to the barn makes our mother nervous, so our father told me to bring her here."

Levi sympathized with a grown woman frustrated by constant supervision, but the threat of danger that loomed made him not only understand her father's caution but also ready to enforce the limits that had been placed on her life. He stepped back and held the door open as he looked at her. "Of course. Come in."

Everett turned to Mandy and motioned with his hand for her to go inside. "Enjoy your day, sister."

She rolled her eyes as she passed Everett and walked into the unfinished house. Their behavior reminded Levi of the siblings' childhood squabbles. Everett jumped down from the porch and was already halfway to the road when Levi closed the door.

She stepped into the front room then turned to him. "I apologize for the disruption to your day. I know you've been working hard to finish your house. I promise not to get in the way. Personally, I believe this constant chaperoning is unnecessary, but Father insists on keeping me under guard. I welcomed it at first, but some days I can't bear the thought of being indoors another moment."

He was more than willing to have her with him— he was delighted—but he kept that to himself. "Your father's right. You can't allow a few weeks of peace to lull you into forgetting about the possibility that Felix and—"

"Oh, I haven't forgotten! Believe me, fear has become my constant companion. Everett was right though: I have started going out by myself, and it's making my parents afraid. I miss my freedom."

"That's understandable."

She looked out the window. "I miss walking to the village whenever I wanted and visiting people and spending Saturdays at the market. Even when I do see anyone besides my family, they act like I'm a leper… as if tragedy is contagious." She looked back at him. "Except you."

He remembered how people acted around him the first few months after his mother was killed. He understood what she was going through—at least in that regard—but he didn't know how to tell her. A drop of water rolled down his face from his wet hair, and he dabbed at it with the towel. "You are welcome here any time."

"Thank you." She grinned slightly then walked to the fireplace and touched the stone mantel. As she wandered around the empty front room examining his work, her hand trailed over the chair rail along the wall. "This is beautiful. You aren't just building a house here, you're crafting something special."

He stood holding the damp towel between his hands, unsure of what to do with her in his house all day. He glanced toward the unfinished kitchen and realized she was his first guest. "I'm still sleeping at home—for Bethany's sake—so I'm afraid I have nothing to offer you. Have you eaten?"

"Yes." Her lips curved. "You don't need to entertain me." She walked to the window and tapped a finger on the new glass then touched the lock on the rail of the sash window. "You must find it tiring to work and worry about your sisters too. I know Connor is with them now, but school will soon be back in session and he won't be able to stay with Lydia all day. At some point we all have to go back to our normal way of life."

"Yes... at some point. I don't want my family living in fear either, but I agree with your father and—as much as I hate to admit it—my father: Felix and Harvey will return soon and we must stay prepared."

He rested a hand on his hip and felt his empty belt loop. He excused himself and walked back through the bedroom and into the washroom to retrieve his belt and shoes. As he stepped back into the bedroom, he saw Mandy in the bedroom doorway. She traced a finger across the unhinged door that leaned against the wall. "Why put a door on your bedroom if you're going to live here alone?"

He lowered his chin as he slipped his belt through the loops on his pants. "Perhaps for privacy while dressing when I have unexpected guests."

Mandy gave a small laugh but seemed otherwise unaffected by her impropriety. She stepped farther into his unfurnished bedroom. "What are we working on today?"

He buckled his belt and scanned the tools and planks of prepared wood stacked around the room. "We? *I* am working on trim and the doors for the kitchen cabinets."

"I can help you."

He felt a smirk coming on but controlled his expression. "With carving and drilling?"

"How do you think instruments are formed?" She arched one thin brow.

He realized how little thought he had given to her work and felt idiotic. "Oh, I'm sorry." He gestured to the tools on the floor. "Please, be my guest."

He spread out the pieces for the cabinet doors and Mandy stepped to the pile of wood. He explained his process and took her into the kitchen to show her his plan. She seemed pleased to work with him and thanked him as she returned to the bedroom. Then she picked up the correct tools and immediately started to work on the cabinet doors.

Levi worked on the trim in the kitchen, and Mandy sat on the floor in the bedroom and carved grooves for hinges in the cabinet doors. Throughout the morning, she brought the doors to him one by one as she completed them. Her carvings were precise and her craftsmanship flawless. She proved not only her skill but also her love for the work.

At midday, as Levi lifted one of the newly finished doors to attach it to the cupboard, he noticed a miniscule carving of a simple smiling face etched on the inside of the door near the hinge. Due to the carving's small size, he held the cabinet door close to the window to inspect the image in the sunlight. The tiny design was deliberately carved. He leaned around the edge of the kitchen wall to look at Mandy. She was sitting in the bedroom beneath the window with her legs straight out along the wooden floor. A cabinet door rested on her lap as she carved the indentions for hinges along its inside edge. She didn't look up at him but was smiling, waiting for his response to the happy carving.

Levi thought of their school days and how often Mandy's playful nature distracted those in the class. What he once found annoying, he now found refreshing. He walked into the bedroom and crouched on the floor beside her. He studied her for a moment before he spoke. "I found your trademark."

"Did you?" She kept her eyes on her work but her grin prevailed.

"Should I assume every new wood instrument in the Land possesses such a carving inside?"

"Only if it's of the highest quality." Mandy blew the wood shavings off the piece she was carving then looked at him and beamed. "Did you like it?"

"I loved it." He dusted a wood shaving from her shoulder. When she didn't flinch, he was tempted to touch her again. Aware of his desire, he pulled his hand away and stood. She looked back at her work and seemed oblivious of her affect, while he was left imagining a life with her, the joy of her constant companionship, waking up beside her every morning, earning her respect, watching her mother their children.

The chisel scraped away one thin sliver of wood at a time as she continued carving. "I hope you notice it again someday when you're a wrinkled, old man and you reach into the cabinet for a coffee cup. Perhaps—if your memory is still intact—you will think of me and smile." She kept talking but remained focused on the cabinet door lying across her lap. She picked up a small piece of sand paper and made a few quick swipes at a rough spot. Then she switched back to the chisel. "Or perhaps your wife will notice it one day and when you tell her it was carved by the scandalous Mandy Foster she will be overcome with jealousy."

He watched her mouth as she spoke and was amazed how she could go for hours without saying a word while she worked and then chatter nonsensically without losing her focus. He leaned his shoulder into the wall and listened to her prattle on. He wondered if interrupting her imaginative tale would break her concentration. "Perhaps I won't tell her."

"Tell whom?" Mandy's hand stopped and she looked up at him.

"My wife." When she only rumpled her brows at his comment, he felt the need to clarify. "You said my future wife would notice your carving one day and she would become jealous—"

"Oh, yes." She laughed. "Right, please, don't tell the poor woman I was involved or you may never have a cup of coffee in peace again."

* * *

Late in the afternoon, Mandy stood from the floor of the empty bedroom in Levi's house where she had spent most of the day carving grooves for hinges into cabinet doors. She brushed the wood shavings from her lap and shook out her skirt, then she carried another cabinet door into his kitchen. He was standing on a footstool hammering a length of quarter round between the upper cabinets and the ceiling. There was still trim left to be secured, and he only had one nail held between his lips. She bent to a bucket of finishing nails on the floor and drew out a handful. Levi took the last nail from his lips and hammered it into the trim. Then he looked down at her while she held the nails up to him. His gaze moved from her face to the nails then back to her face again. He took the nails from her palm and grinned but didn't say a word.

As Mandy walked back into the bedroom, she thought about how comfortably they had worked together throughout the day. It surprised her and—at first—she wasn't sure why. She had expected Levi to be private about his work, but he welcomed her help. She had even expected him to denigrate her work, but he was kind and showed appreciation for her craftsmanship.

They were different together now, and she supposed it was a maturity gained from the harrowing experience they had shared only a month and a half before. She thought of the night they spent in confession in the back of the wagon. She had been so grateful he rescued her that she shared her biggest secret, and it changed everything between them. Without a selfish motive, she now respected him, and after nearly losing her, he no longer acted resentful toward her. She was enjoying his friendship, but it only filled her with regret; long ago she had turned down the one man she could have easily spent her life with, and now she was considered ruined and he would never declare his love again.

After Mandy selected the next piece of wood to carve, she sat on the floor. Her stomach growled and she glanced out the window, guessing the hour. Then she heard Levi's footsteps on the dusty wood floor, and she looked up at him.

Levi combed his hair with his fingers. "Let's go."

"Where?"

"To my house—or, rather, my family's house. It will be dinnertime soon. Aren't you hungry?"

Her stomach growled again as she laid the wood on the floor. She brushed her hands together. "Yes, I am."

He offered his hand and helped her up. Then he pointed to the stack of wood that was a fraction of what it had been when she arrived that morning. "We've accomplished a lot together."

"Yes, we have." She smiled at him and stepped out of the bedroom. The house smelled of fresh lumber with a faint masculine undertone. She walked to the front door and stopped there, expecting the same routine her father and Everett performed before they let her outdoors. She waited while Levi stepped to the window. He looked out in every direction then he moved to the door. He unlocked it and stepped out first. After he glanced again from side to side, he waved her out.

Mandy felt tired of being guarded. As she walked out the door and onto his front porch, she looked at Levi. "I remember when our doors were left open during good weather. I miss it."

He reached behind her and pulled the door closed. "So do I."

While they walked across Levi's property and onto the road, Mandy took his arm. "This is the first time I have walked this road since—" She stopped herself. She was tired of talking about it, tired of thinking about it, and determined not to ruin a pleasant stroll to the village by bringing it up. He glanced at her then behind them. Though she appreciated his protection, she was eager to think of something else. She drew a deep breath. "Thank you, Levi."

"I'm not sure what for, but you're welcome."

"For letting me stay with you today."

"I think you earned your keep."

"We worked well together, didn't we?"

"Yes, I noticed." Levi grinned but still looked straight ahead. "You surprised me."

"What do you mean?"

He only shrugged in response. She found his willingness to comment but his lack of elaboration curious. Before the attack his comments to her were rare and usually caustic; she dismissed them without wanting explanation. But since he had shown a change of attitude toward her, she found his kindness enthralling and wished he would open up and talk more than he did.

Levi stopped walking and reached for something in the grass beside the road. He stood and held out a little yellow daisy to her. She took it and smiled at his sweet gesture, but she said nothing as they continued to walk down the road.

Soon the entrance to the Colburn property came into view. The large old house peeked through the treetops. Mandy had spent as much time in that house as a child as she had in her own. "I suppose it's natural that we work well together—after being friends for so long." Even as Mandy said it, she knew it wasn't quite true. Whatever was between them now was new. She began to contemplate it then shook her head, determined not to allow the notion to tempt her to hope for his affection. There could be nothing more between them. She could only savor the sweetness of his friendship. He was a good man and building his own home. He wouldn't remain unattached for long, and she doubted his future wife would appreciate frequent visits from a salaciously reputed female friend. She resolved simply to enjoy his company while she could.

Levi was quiet as they left the road and walked on the Colburn property. Then as they approached the house, he glanced at her and said, "I suppose." And she realized he had been thinking about their relationship that whole time, too.

* * *

Mandy let go of Levi's arm and stepped into the Colburn kitchen as he held the back door open for her. She glanced back at him and smiled, wishing their time alone could have lasted a little longer. Lydia popped out of the pantry holding a broom. She greeted them and then disappeared back inside. Connor called to Levi from the parlor. Mandy watched Levi go into the other room as she walked through the open kitchen to the pantry. She stopped at the pantry door and looked inside. The small room was lit only by the afternoon sunlight that came from nearby windows. Lydia had several bushel baskets pulled into the center of the pantry's stone floor, and she was sweeping the area behind them.

Lydia smiled as her eyes drifted down Mandy's wrinkled and dusty dress. "I take it you've been working in your shop today."

"I've been working all day but not at home." She stepped inside the pantry and moved the baskets back into place after Lydia swept. "I was at Levi's house."

Lydia's straw broom paused briefly then continued sweeping. "You and Everett?"

"No. Just me."

The broom stopped. "You and Levi were alone all day …at his house?"

Mandy nodded.

"What will your parents think when they hear that?" Lydia's symmetrical eyebrows lifted as she voiced her concern for the breach of custom.

"It was my father's idea. He had Everett take me there so I wouldn't walk from the house to my workshop unguarded." She rolled her eyes.

"They're just trying to protect you."

"I know. I'm just sick of it."

"Me too." Lydia's expression changed and she set the broom against the shadowed wall. "I didn't see Levi's face when he came in. Was he… pleasant?"

Mandy leaned out of the pantry to see if the kitchen was still vacant then turned back to Lydia. "He was quite pleasant. We both were. We spent the day working on his kitchen cupboards. I truly enjoyed being with him. We worked surprisingly well together."

"He loves you, Mandy. You must know that."

Mandy shook her head. "I know how he used to think of me, but everything is different between us now. We have both changed. I no longer want the intrigue I once did, and he is no longer resentful toward me. We are both without pretense and... it feels good."

Lydia's smile curved up at the edges and she stepped closer. "Do you love him?"

"Of course I love him—he is a dear friend. But I can't allow myself to think beyond that because I know he would never have me now."

Lydia chuckled. "And why not?"

"Because he knows about my past."

Lydia moved around Mandy and checked the kitchen's emptiness for herself then whirled back around. "How does he know? I never uttered a word, I promise."

"I confessed it myself."

"You told him about—"

"The shearer? Yes."

Lydia pressed her palm to her stomach and glanced toward the parlor. "How did he react?"

"He promised never to speak of it—and I trust him." She could hear Levi and Connor talking and laughing with Bethany in the parlor. It sounded like Connor was teaching Bethany more of his card tricks. Still, she lowered her voice. "I know Levi wouldn't want me for a wife now, and I understand. I'm satisfied with his friendship, but I do regret my past— not only my indiscretion but also how I treated him. I told him that after he rescued me and he was quick to forgive. Everything I went through changed me somehow and I no longer crave attention, but I am growing fond of Levi... very fond of him."

"I know my brother and he loves you. If you love him, he deserves to know." Lydia played with the gold band around her finger as she looked at Mandy. "If he gave you a second chance, would you reject him again?"

"He would not."

"*If* he did?"

"No, I wouldn't reject him. I love him—" As Mandy acknowledged the depth of her love for Levi, she was struck by the torrent of affection she had tried to ignore. She held up a hand when Lydia started to smile. "But I can't think that way anymore. I know the tradition and Levi wouldn't marry me." Mandy leaned her head against the pantry door and sighed. "I know the emptiness inside me has a purpose. I used to try to fill it, but not anymore. I may regret my past, but I'm at peace with my circumstances. I truly am."

Lydia's persistent smile left little hope that the matter would be forgotten. It made Mandy nervous. She lowered her chin. "Lydia, please don't say anything to him."

"I won't say anything... outright. But if he asks me, I will be forced to encourage him—out of my love for both of you, of course." Lydia bent to a basket of potatoes and handed several to Mandy. Then Lydia grabbed a handful of green beans. She walked out of the pantry to the kitchen sink and Mandy followed her. As she set the potatoes in the sink, Lydia pointed to the bottom of Mandy's dress. "I can cook dinner. You need to go to the washroom upstairs and make yourself presentable."

* * *

While eating dinner in the Colburns' kitchen, Mandy felt a strange sort of tension among everyone at the table. She tried not to look directly at Lydia, who was seated across from her, because every time their eyes met, Lydia glanced at Levi and back at her and then grinned with obvious delight. John Colburn was out for the evening—meeting with the village elders—and Mandy enjoyed the casual nature of the meal, though the aged Isabella was eager to use the absence of John's authority to press the Colburn siblings on personal matters. After she questioned Lydia on her and Connor's plans to have children, she critiqued Levi's life choices. Then Isabella turned her attention to Mandy. "Miss Foster, I was thrilled indeed to hear how Levi rescued you during that terrible ordeal. He proved to be quite the hero, didn't he?"

"Yes, Miss Colburn."

"Call me Aunt Isabella, dear." The elderly woman chewed a bite of food then swallowed and pointed her fork at Levi. "So is he your hero then?"

Mandy felt her cheeks warm as Bethany, Lydia, and Connor all smiled and widened their eyes, enjoying Isabella's intrusive questioning. She didn't dare glance at Levi, who was sitting beside her. "Yes, I suppose he is," she answered then looked at Lydia and shrugged.

Isabella ate quietly for a moment. Mandy took her last bite of food and laid her fork across the top of her plate. She thought the questions had ended and began to relax when Isabella turned her head toward her again. "Have you any suitors currently, Miss Foster?"

"Pardon?"

"Suitors, Miss Foster? Have you a suitor at present?"

Mandy glanced at Connor when she saw him grin at Levi. She folded her hands in her lap. "No." She pressed her lips together and hoped a curt answer would encourage someone to change the subject. She was too embarrassed to look beside her at Levi. She was sure he was equally uncomfortable. However, the rest of them seemed to be enjoying the show.

"You hear that, Levi?" Isabella grinned as she spoke. "You are her hero and she has no suitor. What do you make of that?"

"Nothing, Aunt Isabella. I make nothing of it." Levi set his fork on his plate and stood. He collected his empty plate and Mandy's and carried the dishes to the sink.

Bethany snickered, and it drew Isabella's attention. "And you, sweet Bethany. Next year you will turn eighteen, and I believe the men in this village are quite familiar with your father's rule about his daughters not courting until age eighteen."

"Aunt Isabella—" Bethany whined but it didn't stop her great-aunt's observations.

"Oh, this house will be swarming with young men then. I will have to swing my cane in all directions to keep them away from you."

Levi turned back to the table. He grinned in Bethany's direction, and then he motioned with his hand toward Mandy. "Come, Mandy. I will walk you home."

As Mandy followed Levi out, she heard Bethany giggle. She waited until they were on the road before she took Levi's arm. The setting sun left pink streaks across the sky over the ocean. Though out of the house, the onset of evening made her sigh as she glanced to the west.

Levi looked too. "The sunset is beautiful, isn't it?"

"I guess." She looked away from the sky and stared at the road ahead.

"What do you mean *you guess*? I thought all women loved the sunset. My sisters all say it's romantic."

"Not to me. I always get sad when the sun sets. It used to happen only when I was alone, but now it's all the time." She could feel Levi looking at her, so she glanced at him and grinned, hoping he wouldn't think her insane. "It's strange, I know. It just makes me feel sort of empty. I used to try to fill that emptiness with anything that made the feeling go away. But after the attack, I realized the emptiness had a purpose. I'm trying to learn to listen to it and not yearn for things that can't be."

Levi glanced over his shoulder and scanned their surroundings as the last light of day barely lit their path. Then he looked at her; his brow creased and his eyes were full of concern. "What do you yearn for that can't be?"

Mandy shrugged. "The same things every woman my age wants, I suppose: a husband and a family of my own. But it doesn't matter... I have to protect my family from my past. I never thought it would bother me, but time seems to be moving faster now, and I see how short life is."

Levi stopped on the road and Mandy thought something was wrong. Her pulse quickened. But he only bent to the ground and picked a little yellow daisy like the one he had given her earlier in the day. He looked at the flower for a moment, then handed it to her and continued walking.

Mandy took the tiny flower and glanced up at Levi. "Why?"

"Hm?"

"Why these little daisies?"

"I don't know. I like them."

Mandy chuckled. "The biggest man in the village likes the tiniest flower. Why?"

"They're delicate and... I don't know." Levi grinned at her briefly, then he looked down the road and his smile faded. "My mother liked them. When I was little I would pick them for her and she would smile so big when I gave them to her. The day she... the day Felix and his sons... that was the last thing I had given her. She was in the kitchen putting the little flower in a tiny vase when they came in."

"I'm sorry. I didn't know."

Levi cleared his throat. "I've never told anyone before."

Mandy looked down at the little flower and then up at the grown man who had picked it. "You don't think it was your fault do you?"

"What do you mean?"

"Your mother was in the kitchen putting the flower you gave her in a vase and that is where she was attacked. You don't blame yourself, do you?"

"No, of course not. I know who killed her." His arm stiffened beneath her hand. "And I'm not going to let him take anyone else away from me ever again."

CHAPTER TEN

Levi stayed at the breakfast table and sipped his coffee long after the others had finished eating. One by one his family members left the kitchen. As Lydia cleared the table, she pointed at the coffee pot in front of Levi. He shook his head. She left it there and took the other dishes to the sink.

Connor came in the back door sweaty from his morning run. He kissed Lydia then sat at the table and held an empty coffee cup in front of Levi. Levi picked up the coffee pot and filled the cup, then refilled his own cup for the third time. Lydia finished the dishes and said she was going to check on Isabella.

Connor lifted a finger to the coffee pot as he looked at Levi. "Long night?"

Levi yawned and rubbed his forehead with his fingertips. "I stared at the ceiling until sunrise."

"Would this have anything to do with your date yesterday?"

"My what?" He had grown accustomed to most of Connor's expressions, but still preferred an explanation. Connor simply lifted his brow in response.

Levi nodded. He didn't feel like talking about it, but a day alone with Mandy in his house had made one thing clear to him—he loved her and still wanted her to be his wife. "I have to do what's best for her."

"And what's that?"

Levi thought of how—after her abduction—she said she no longer wanted to be desired by any man and that she couldn't have the things she yearned for because she wanted to keep her past a secret. It took constant effort for him to put his feelings aside, and when he did it only made him love her more. He told himself she was only comfortable with him because she felt safely undesired. "She trusts me. I am not going to betray her trust." He thought of their time working together in his house—it had felt natural having her there with him. He had spent the long night trying not to imagine a life with Mandy in the house he was building for her.

Connor tipped his coffee cup high, drinking the last drop, then he set it on the table. He lowered his chin as he looked at Levi. "I remember the exact moment with Lydia when I realized I would either marry her or move far away and never see her again. I knew that anything in between would kill me."

"I felt that way about Mandy for six years." Levi blew out a breath. "But not anymore."

"I see... so you're over her?" Connor's sarcasm came with a chuckle.

"No, but everything is different between us now." There was a light knock on the kitchen door. Thankful for the diversion, Levi left the table to answer it. He opened the door but didn't see anyone. He looked down the path to Lydia's cottage where a boy was knocking on the medical office door. "Are you looking for Doctor Bradshaw?"

The boy ran back to the kitchen door. "No, I need Mr. Bradshaw."

Levi stepped back and looked at Connor. "Someone is here to see you."

As Connor moved to the door, Levi returned to the table. He overheard the boy pant a description of something he said had washed ashore, but he didn't hear the details.

Connor nodded to the boy. "Tell your father not to touch it. We'll be right there."

The boy ran away and Connor turned to Levi. "His dad found something on the beach and he thinks it's from the outside world. I'll tell John we're leaving. Grab some gloves and come with me."

* * *

The morning sun climbed steadily in the eastern sky over the ocean. Its rays reflected off the water in blinding splinters of light. Levi squinted as he walked the well-worn path through the edge of the forest to the shore. As he and Connor approached the small crowd that had formed on the beach, Levi saw the strange hunk of twisted metal protruding from the sand. Golden mirrored plates were linked together in precise rows of geometric patterns, framed by metal poles, and anchored to a dome-shaped object that jutted from the sand like an upended bathtub. Fierce burn marks scarred most of its surface.

Several young boys gathered around the object. Their curious fingers pointed at the shiny conglomeration of warped metal and unfamiliar materials. Connor convinced them not to handle it. He explained that people in other lands sent scientific instruments into space. He said it was common for those objects to land unexpectedly on other parts of the earth. Levi only took his eyes off the strange mass long enough to see the blank looks of confusion on the boys' faces. He did his best to appear as though he understood Connor's explanation, if only to bolster their trust in the Land's only outsider.

Connor removed a glove and held his hand close to the metal but didn't touch it. "It's not giving off any heat." He looked at the man who had discovered it and raised his voice above the sound of the waves. "When did you first see it?"

The man shrugged. "A few minutes ago. I sent my son to get you as soon as we spotted it."

Connor knelt in front of the mass. He slipped his hand back into the glove and began to scoop sand away from the part of the object that extended into the earth. Levi knelt beside him and helped him dig. It had symbols along its edge. He pointed to a group of marks. "What are these symbols?"

Connor stopped digging and studied the marks. "Letters—well, characters actually."

"What does it say?"

"I don't know. I don't read much Chinese."

They dug deeper into the sand and then stopped again. Levi looked at the beach between the ocean and the object and noticed that the sand was relatively undisturbed. "This didn't wash in with the tide—not today anyway."

Connor nodded. "I think it's been here for a while—at least a day or so." He took off his glove and touched a metal piece with the back of his hand. "It's cold. And you're right: it didn't wash in from the ocean."

"Where do you think it came from?"

"The sky."

Levi stood and his eyes followed the structure a few inches above his head. He glanced into the sky above and saw nothing but blue and a few cottony clouds. He looked back at the metal mass. "What is it?"

Connor walked around the object, studying it before he replied. Levi followed and watched Connor, waiting for his answer. Connor glanced back at the onlookers, then he looked at Levi and lowered his voice. "It's space debris—probably part of a satellite." He touched a section of the reflective geometric plates. "These look like part of a newer-styled solar array, so there's probably no threat of radioactive material, but I still don't want people touching it."

Levi heard him say there was no threat of something, but he could tell by Connor's face that the mass still posed some danger. Levi looked back at the boys. "Go get the overseer."

As the boys ran toward the Colburn house, Levi scanned the shore around them. A thought occurred to him, and he nudged Connor. "This is the exact spot where you landed."

Connor nodded. "Same time of year, too. Yesterday was the equinox."

Levi brushed the sand off his gloves and tried to look unconcerned. He glanced at the onlookers and kept his voice quiet. "Do you think it's a coincidence?"

"I don't know. The founders also arrived on the equinox." Connor looked toward the village and back at Levi. "Where on the beach did the founders' ship run aground?"

"Here...exactly here." Levi pointed to a cairn near the tree line. "That pile of stones is the marker." He didn't know what Connor was insinuating, but the thought of a pattern of entry to the Land made his stomach tighten. "What do you think it means?"

"I'm not sure. Maybe the atmospheric phenomenon around the Land is permeable in this one particular place, on one particular day of the year. Or it may not mean anything. Three arrivals in one hundred sixty-something years—that isn't really enough to base a theory on." Connor lifted his chin toward the path from the village, and Levi glanced up to see the boys leading John to them. Everett was walking behind them.

While Connor pointed to various parts of the debris and explained it to John, Everett stood by Levi and looked on. Levi removed his gloves as he glanced at Everett. "Where is Mandy?"

"She's at home."

"With your father?"

"Yes. I came to spar with Connor today..." Everett pointed at the debris. "But this is far more interesting."

Levi nodded. He looked back at the hunk of metal, but his mind was on Mandy's safety. Though he wouldn't say it aloud, he didn't believe Samuel could protect her if Harvey and Felix came back. He often heard Samuel complain of his stiff joints and shortness of breath. Everett had spent over a year learning to fight with Connor. If Everett wasn't with her, Levi wanted to guard Mandy himself. He glanced at the other men there on the beach and realized Bethany and Lydia were at home unprotected. They were his sisters and yet he had thought of Mandy first.

John shielded his eyes with his hand while he listened to Connor explain the satellite's parts and functions. Connor waved Levi closer and Everett followed. John looked at Levi. "Connor says we should dismantle it and remove it from the shore, and I agree. We don't want children playing on it and getting hurt. He suggests we disassemble it here and haul the pieces to the old shed behind our barn."

"I can help," Everett offered.

John put his hand on Everett's shoulder. "Thank you, Everett, but your family needs you more right now."

Turning to the onlookers, John raised his voice over the ocean's sounds and told them all what Connor believed the object was and to leave it alone. Then he turned back to Levi. "Will you help Connor dismantle and move all of this?"

"Of course, Father."

"Good. I need to go back to the house." John nodded then turned to the crowd and shepherded them away from the shore.

Levi watched as the crowd followed his father to the path that led to the village. Then—while Connor stayed with the debris—Levi left the beach to get the tools they needed for the job. On his way he overheard his father tell the curious villagers the debris was only rubbish that had washed ashore and it was nothing to worry about. Levi thought of the coincidence of the place and date and wondered what the villagers would think of the overseer if they knew of his potential mistakenness.

As Levi approached the Colburn property, he diverged from the path and walked to the barn. He gathered every pair of pliers and cutters he could find, along with screwdrivers, spades, and a crowbar. He piled the tools on a long wooden cart and pulled it back to the shore.

* * *

After a day of dismantling the sharp and heavy satellite debris and hauling it away from the shore, Levi wedged the wooden cart into the damp-smelling shed at the back of the Colburn property. Connor walked in behind the cart with his arms full of tools. Levi struck a match and lit the lantern hanging from a nail on the wall in the darkened outbuilding. The light was dim but adequate to finish the work.

As he unloaded the cart, Levi felt the fatigue in his back. Normally, he thrived on tackling large amounts of repetitive work, but after a sleepless night, the long day of disassembling debris under the sun had exhausted him. He handed the last length of metal pole to Connor, who was stacking the pieces of debris in a specific way on the ground along the shed wall.

Levi sat on the empty wooden cart, took off his gloves, and lay back, allowing his head to rest against the cart's sandy bed. "How deep do you think it goes into the sand?"

"I have no idea," Connor replied as he crouched near a pile of solar collectors. "We will probably be at this for a few more days. Are you okay with that?"

"Yes." Levi rubbed his eyes with the heels of his hands.

"Hello?" a female voice came from outside the shed. Levi pulled his hands off his eyes and looked at the door.

"In here," Connor answered as he stood from the floor. His head nearly touched the shed's low ceiling. "Oh, hi Mandy."

Levi sat up as Mandy stepped into the shed. Connor glanced at Levi then dropped the metal pole onto a pile of others. It clanked and rolled to the dirt floor. "I'm going to go inside. The rest of this can wait until morning." He grinned at Levi, then he moved past Mandy and left the shed.

Mandy stepped to the debris piles on the dirt floor. "I came to see the strange materials everyone is talking about. I hope I didn't interrupt your work."

"No. We're done for the night." Levi remained seated on the cart and watched as she bent to inspect the metal. He told himself it was the fatigue, but he felt aggravated at her for walking outside alone at night. "Did you come here by yourself?"

She glanced at him and her smile faded. "My father came as well."

"Out here? To the shed?"

"No, he is in the house speaking with your father."

"Mandy…" Levi shook his head then leaned forward resting his elbows on his knees. "I don't want you wandering around outside by yourself."

"I walked from the house to the shed. That's hardly wandering." She straightened her back. "I was perfectly safe."

"Have you forgotten where you were when you were attacked?"

She raised her eyebrows. He waited for a reaction, but she remained silent. He couldn't read her expression in the dim lantern light, but he wanted to reinforce the potential danger so she would be more careful. "You shouldn't have come out here by yourself."

"My father knew I was coming out here and he had no objection." She crossed her arms.

"Then he was careless."

"Would you so dishonor an elder?"

Levi threw up both hands. "I mean no insolence to your father, but you shouldn't have walked outside in the dark alone."

"I am more frightened by the thought of spending my life trapped indoors than I am of walking in the dark." Her voice grew louder with each word. "I refuse to be held captive any longer."

The return of Mandy's temper exacerbated his frustration. He stood in response to her challenging demeanor but kept his voice low. "I have gone to great lengths to protect you, and I will continue to do so."

"For how long, Levi?"

"Until Felix and Harvey return."

"And what if they don't?"

"They will." He pushed his hand through his hair. Though she was no longer intentionally provocative, she had not lost the ability to move him. "And when they do, I want to know you are somewhere safe. We have to stay prepared."

"By making me hide for the rest of my life?" Mandy's volume increased, giving her voice its old, familiar fullness. "I'm a person, Levi. You can't expect me to remain locked away all the time. I feel caged by all the doors and locks and guards. I haven't forgotten what happened to me. I think about it every second of the day, but I can't live like this anymore!"

"I just want to protect you."

"You want to control me!"

Levi opened his mouth to form an angry response, but he stopped himself and bit back his words. He turned to the door and took a steadying breath, hoping to settle his nerves. He was tired and frustrated, and he didn't want to fight with her. He remembered how broken she was after the attack—he had wanted her restored and strengthened. Somehow he had forgotten with her strength came a fiery independence. He loved her—even the fervor embedded in her nature—but he didn't see how he could protect her without her cooperation. He rubbed the back of his tired neck as he turned to her. "I want to keep you safe. If I'm trying to control you, it's only for your own good."

Mandy narrowed her eyes. "It's not your place."

Her words stung, and he tried to conceal his hurt. No matter how he felt, it was true: she wasn't his to protect. "You're right, Amanda... you are still under your father's protection—he is responsible for you. I wanted you healed, and now that you are, you no longer need me."

Mandy looked down and pressed her thin fingers into her forehead. A few stray curls fell forward. Then she dropped her hands and looked at Levi. "That's not true. I do need you."

Levi's pulse pounded in his throat. He swallowed hard and stepped closer to her. He watched her face, waiting for some sign she needed him—not for protection—but because she loved him. He stood near her in the dimly lit shed, overwhelmed with the need to hear words from a woman he used to wish would be silent. The low light of the lantern barely illumined her, and the anger had dissipated from her face.

Her voice sounded soft again. "I have not forgotten what you did for me. You saved my life. I could never repay you."

"Repay me?" Levi blew out a breath. "Is that all that's between us—your gratitude?"

Mandy flinched and Levi immediately regretted his tone, but he wanted more from her. He had declared his love for her once and she had rejected him. He wouldn't do it again unless he had some assurance from her that it was what she wanted. When she didn't answer, he took a step closer. "Should I assume your silence means your friendship is only an attempt to repay me for saving you? How about the time we spent working in my house? That felt right, Mandy. It felt right having you there with me. Is there nothing more between us?"

"Of course there is."

"Then say it."

"I can't."

"Yes, you can."

"What do you want to hear? That you're the only man who knows my secret? That you have the power to shame me and my family in front of the whole village? You promised you would never bring that up. You promised, Levi!"

"And I'm not bringing it up now."

"But that's what you mean, isn't it? I'm a whore! I'm a whore and I have to live alone the rest of my life because of it. Well, I've accepted God's forgiveness and I've made peace with the life I have to live, but I don't need you reminding me that my secret lies between us."

"That's not what I meant at all."

"I know you've taken on the burden of watching over me as a favor to my father, but I don't need your protection if it's going to cost me my dignity."

"Your dignity?"

"Yes." Mandy pointed her proud chin toward the door. "I've healed from what happened and I'm determined to carry on, but you want to keep reminding me—"

"Only of the danger you are in, not of your past. I want to forget that as much as you do."

"So it does bother you then?"

"Of course it does." As soon as he said it, Levi knew he had been trapped by her captious question, but it was too late to take it back. He looked away and raked his fingers through his hair. After a moment of icy silence, he blew out the lantern then walked out of the shed and waited by the door for Mandy to come out. "It's time to go inside."

After she moved past him, he closed the door and lowered the latch into place. Even in the dark of night, he could feel her anger. He put his hands into his pockets and kept his eyes on the house as he walked toward it.

Mandy walked beside him and, after a few steps, he felt her hand slip beneath his arm. She was still more frightened in the dark than she had admitted. The dignity she had claimed only moments before had already crumbled. Somehow it was his fault. Now she was touching him. Though her vicissitude left him reeling, her gestures were no longer the obviously flirtatious actions they used to be. He respected her for it, but her subtlety only left him confounded.

When they got to the house, Levi held the back door open for Mandy. His father and Samuel were sitting at the kitchen table discussing the satellite debris with Connor. Mandy moved straight through the kitchen and into the parlor. Connor glanced at Levi, then Mandy, then back at Levi. Levi caught Connor's questioning expression and held up a finger to let him know he would be right back. He stepped through the kitchen and looked into the parlor as he walked to the stairs. Bethany, Everett, and Lydia were reclined on the rug playing cards, while Isabella sat in her chair nearby. Mandy had already curled up next to her brother and appeared unaffected by what had happened in the shed. Levi caught Lydia's eye, then he climbed the stairs, taking the steps two at a time.

Levi rounded the upstairs landing and walked down the hallway and into his bedroom. He closed the door behind him with more force than he intended. He needed to change his sand-caked shirt and go back downstairs where the men were discussing the satellite debris, but the argument with Mandy repeated in his mind and distracted him. He tried to focus on the routine task of changing clothes and stepped to his dresser to retrieve a clean shirt. As he did, he imagined Mandy in the shed—first pleasant, then bellicose, then silent—and wondered how any man could keep up with such volatility. He slipped his arms into the sleeves of the fresh shirt and sat on the edge of his bed while he buttoned it. As he reached down to remove his shoes, a knock on the door interrupted his thoughts. He glared at the door. "What?"

The door opened a few inches and Lydia tilted her head into view. "I thought you looked upset when you passed through the parlor. Are you all right?"

"No."

Lydia stepped into the room, leaving the door cracked slightly. He pointed to it and Lydia closed the door all the way.

"I thought something had changed between me and Mandy, but I was wrong. I don't know what she wants." Levi looked at his hands as he spoke. He rubbed the scar on his palm with the thumb of the other hand. Whenever he looked at it, he thought of Mandy. "She came out to the shed to see the debris and we got in an argument."

When Lydia didn't respond, Levi looked up at her and saw his sister was smiling. His problem wasn't funny. "Are you amused by my agony?"

"Levi, she didn't go out to the shed to see the debris—she went out there to see you." Lydia sat beside him on the bed. "If you knew Mandy loved you, would you give her a second chance?"

Levi snapped his head toward his sister. "If you know something, you must tell me."

"I can't tell you anything." She spoke slowly as if giving a secret message. "Just answer the question: if you knew she loved you, would you give her a second chance?"

"If I *knew* she loved me?"

"Yes. If you knew she loved you, would you court her?"

"No."

Lydia drew her head back. "No?"

"No—if I knew she loved me, I would marry her." He pressed his lips together and shook his head. "But she doesn't want that. After the attack, she said she never wants to be desired by any man ever again. Then things changed between us—we started responding to each other differently. We worked together yesterday—in my house, hanging cabinet doors—and I loved every minute of it. I can honestly say that was the best day of my life. I was awake all night thinking about it... thinking about her. I thought something new had formed between us, but I was wrong. She is just grateful I saved her and she thinks I'm protecting her to help her father."

"You can't give up on her so easily." Lydia's smile returned.

"Don't encourage me with encrypted signals." He chuckled out of frustration rather than amusement. "I don't need another woman trying to confuse me."

"Then I will advise you plainly: if you don't know what she wants—and you truly love her—you must ask her." Lydia stood and walked to the door. Before she opened it she glanced over her shoulder at him. "I am bound by friendship to remain silent about her feelings, and she is bound by tradition. You are the only one who is silent by choice. Perhaps you should rethink that choice."

* * *

After Lydia left the room, Levi sat motionless on the edge the bed. He would have no peace while his mind churned as it did. He was in love—beyond intrigue—with a woman who claimed she didn't want to be loved. She had said so herself, but he no longer believed her.

He thought about Lydia's insinuation that the choice was his. He certainly didn't feel like he had a choice in the matter. If Mandy loved him but was disregarding her feelings, his choices seemed limited. Lydia had said Mandy was bound by tradition. He wondered what that meant. He couldn't imagine why she would forgo his affection if she felt the same way, unless she believed he wouldn't have her because of her past. Though the traditions of the Land dictated he should shun her, he wouldn't reject her. Surely Mandy knew he would never reject her. If she didn't know, he understood how that fear could compel her to silence.

The realization sent a sudden jolt through his core. He stood to pace the small bedroom that he had slept in his entire life. He didn't care about any tradition that would keep him from the woman he loved or that would cause her shame. She had confessed and changed—he could think of no further demand any tradition should place on a person. She had said no good man would have her now, but he would—and not conciliatorily to avert a life alone, but with the honor of redeeming a precious treasure.

In his mind Levi answered Lydia's question again—if Mandy loved him, yes, he would indeed give her a second chance. But first he would have to find a way to marry her without the village's tradition exposing her past and shaming her family. He charged out of his room, renewed in hope, and shuffled down the stairs into the empty parlor. Confused by the vacant room, Levi stepped into the kitchen. Connor stood at the stove drawing a ladle full of stew from a large pot. The back door was closed.

Levi walked to the stove. "Where is everyone?"

Connor emptied the ladle into a bowl. He held the bowl of stew out to Levi. "The Fosters went home. Someone needed Lydia, and since I hadn't eaten yet, your dad was kind enough to go with her to her office. Bethany and Isabella went to their rooms, last I knew. What's up?"

"I wanted to be in on your meeting with my father and Samuel, but it looks like I'm too late." Levi accepted the bowl of stew. Connor picked up another bowl for himself then filled it and went to the table.

Levi had not realized how hungry he was until he began to eat. As the nutrients replenished his energy, he thought of his day's work. He lifted his chin toward Connor. "So what did my father and Samuel have to say about the debris?"

"Not much. They were hoping I had the answers, but I haven't come to any conclusions yet." Connor leaned back in his chair and picked up his water glass. He took a drink and lowered the glass to the table but didn't let it go. His usual positive demeanor clouded over when he spoke of the potential the threat of the outside world. He scowled at the glass and swirled the water around and around as he formed his thoughts. "I mentioned the coincidence that part of a satellite landed in the exact spot at the exact time of the year I landed here and the founders' ship ran ashore here."

"What did they think of it?"

"Your dad was concerned, but he agreed that's all it is at this point—a coincidence." Connor set the glass down. "I still believe there is some kind of atmospheric phenomenon that makes the Land undetectable to the outside world. That's my best guess simply because as an aviator I flew over the South Atlantic Ocean many times and never saw land here. The Land isn't visible on satellite images or apparently by search crews. I know the Unified States Navy would have searched for me after the jet crash, but we never saw any of that activity from here. Still, undetectable doesn't mean impermeable. I've considered the possibility that whatever protects the Land is weakened somehow at the equinox, but that can't be confirmed by only three arrivals in seven generations. And all three entries were in March—the autumn equinox here on the Southern Hemisphere—

so that makes me wonder if the earth's orbital position matters also."

Levi kept eating while he listened. He was amazed he had learned enough from Connor in two years to follow what he said.

Connor leaned his elbows on the table and rubbed his thumbs across his brow. "I want to be able to say confidently what is happening and how we can protect this place, but all I can do is speculate. I still chart the stars every clear night, and by the patterns during the last two years I'm certain the atmosphere over the Land is altered, but how and why—I can't say. It's like there is a protective bubble over this place—or at least I really want there to be. I've lived out there. The world war made the planet almost unlivable two years ago. I can't imagine what life is like out there now. But I promise you this: we don't want whatever is out there coming in here." He sighed and dropped his hands to the table's edge. "This place is my home now. I have a wife and we're trying to start a family. Believe me, I want to have the answers for the elders... more than answers, I want to have a plan to protect the Land."

Levi pushed his empty soup bowl away and drummed his fingers on the table. He understood the threat brought by the fallen debris but had no idea what they could do about it. He trusted his brother-in-law's judgment and would agree to whatever Connor decided in the matter. "What kind of a plan do you have in mind?"

"That's just it, if a sailboat runs ashore with a few guys on it, I think we can manage—depending on their weaponry and attitudes. But if an aircraft carrier with a crew of five thousand pulls up ready to take over…" He raised both hands.

"Do you think either of those scenarios is likely?"

Connor shrugged. "I truly believe the Land is undetectable. The founders were on the only vessel ever to arrive by sea, and that was a total accident. But if another vessel was positioned in the right place, at the right time, maybe it could run aground here too."

"What could we do to defend the Land?"

Connor shifted in his chair then grinned confidently. "I know what you would want to do."

"Fight?" Levi chuckled. "Yes, but even I know when I'm outnumbered."

"Your dad wants a plan that begins with diplomatic attempts."

"Of course he does." Levi smirked.

Connor lifted a finger. "He's a peacemaker. That's just his nature."

Levi's stomach drew into a tight knot. "His peaceful nature killed my mother."

"No, Felix killed your mother."

"My father did nothing about it."

Connor raised a palm. "He says he regrets it."

"That's not good enough."

"He has apologized to you. What else do you want him to do?"

"There's nothing he could do to make me forgive him." Levi looked away. He wished he could be like Connor and everyone else and see his father as a noble widower—a good man who lost his wife, but he couldn't let it go, and he was tired of talking about it.

He leaned back in his chair. "So what if someone from the outside world did find the Land? What do you think we should do?"

Connor looked at his water glass. "In the case of a large scale invasion, my first thought is to have an evacuation plan for the whole village."

"Where would we go? Inland?"

"Maybe. I don't know how reasonable it is to ask seventy families to load up their wagons and drive their livestock toward the mountains. Then there are all the other villages to consider. Even if Good Springs is the point of entry for the Land, modern land vehicles could make it all the way to Southpoint or Northcrest in a few hours. The enemy would get to the other villages before we could warn everyone."

Levi shook his head. "Very few people in Good Springs understand how you got here and what the outside world is like. You saw the looks on the people's faces today when you told them not to touch the space debris. That's how they would look at you if you told them to load up their families and leave their homes." Levi imagined it and leaned forward. "Especially if you mention going toward the mountains. People are afraid of the mountains."

"Because of Felix?"

"No. Felix's ancestors were sent west—or so the story goes. Father says they settled somewhere near the mountains, but they didn't cross the mountains. Obviously, they live somewhere out there. I have never stopped Felix to ask him where exactly. But even before Felix attacked, people were afraid of the mountains. I always heard no one has gone over them and returned to tell about it."

Connor nodded. "So it doesn't seem like evacuation would be an option. And we have no defensive weapons—"

Levi held up a fist and grinned.

Connor chuckled. "Useless against modern weapons. Most military vessels could obliterate this village without a single crewman leaving the ship. Maybe your dad is right."

The mention of his father's diplomatic tactics irritated Levi. He took a deep breath and crossed his arms over his chest. "Should we build a tower near the place where the founders ran ashore and—every year on the equinox—sit out there and keep watch?"

"Don't forget I dropped out of the sky, and so did that satellite debris. If anyone is in a watchtower, I suggest they look up." Connor shook his head. "Like I said—I don't have the answers. All I can do is drag the debris into the shed and hope we can make something useful out of it."

CHAPTER ELEVEN

Mandy folded a dishtowel in half and pulled a hot pan of biscuits from the oven. She closed the oven door and dropped the pan onto the stovetop with a clang. Moving around her mother, she reached into the cupboard for plates. She wondered if the casual dinner would include the whole Colburn household and looked at her mother. "Seven or eight?"

Roseanna plopped a chunk of butter onto her best butter dish and shook her head. "Just the four of us and John. Isabella says she is too tired to go out in the evenings, and Connor and Lydia are enjoying time to themselves." She glanced at the darkened kitchen window. "Everett should be finished in the barn soon. I told him we're having company."

Mandy reached into the cupboard and took down five plates. "What about Bethany?"

"She's sleeping at her friend's house tonight." Roseanna took the butter to the table and wiped her hands on her apron as she walked back to Mandy. "John didn't mention Levi—maybe he's coming, too. Go ahead and set six places."

Mandy's stomach fluttered. She had not seen Levi since their argument in the shed a week prior and had relived their conversation many times in her mind. Each mental reenactment presented a new angle and a new set of emotions. He had asked if she felt only gratitude toward him, and she had failed to answer. Now she regretted it. Lydia had advised her to tell him how she felt, but Mandy knew he would be obligated to reject her because of her past. But the more she thought about it, the more she wondered if Lydia were right: even if Levi rejected her, he deserved to know how she felt. He had loved her for years, and he had saved her life. If he rejected her, she would add that to the mountain of punishment her choices had already accrued.

As Mandy set the places at the table, her father opened the front door. She held her breath as Samuel let John in the house, but Levi wasn't with him. Roseanna nudged her. "Sorry, Amanda. I shouldn't have raised your hopes."

Mandy walked back to the stove. As she pulled the biscuits from the pan and piled them into a basket, she glanced at her mother. "Am I that obvious?"

"You are to me, darling, but probably not to Levi, or he would be here."

Mandy tried to ignore the downward pull of regret. She felt caged in the hot kitchen and fanned her face with her hands as she stepped away from the stove. She listened to her father and John conversing in the parlor and decided to confirm Levi's absence for herself. She stepped around the corner and looked into the parlor where the men sat in armchairs near the unlit fireplace. Framing her mouth with a polite smile, she interrupted their conversation. "Excuse me, Father, Mr. Colburn. Are we just waiting for Everett, or will Levi be joining us as well?"

John shook his head. "Levi was anxious to get back to work after spending a week hauling debris from the shore. I have not seen him today. I assume he is still working at his house." He tilted his head a degree and looked at her with the intense gaze he used when he detected deeper desires. "I apologize for his absence."

Mandy realized her smile had wilted, and she tried her best to bring it back. Her father glanced up at her. Immediately, she turned and walked to the kitchen, feeling exposed.

Roseanna kept the food warm a while longer and waited for Everett. Finally, she paced to the window, heaved a sigh, and said they should go ahead and eat. Samuel and John came into the kitchen and sat at either end of the table. Mandy sat across from her mother and between two empty chairs. She could hear Shep in front of the house barking and wondered when Everett would come inside. John prayed before the food was served, and in the brief silence between *Amen* and the chorus of clinking knives and serving spoons, Mandy heard something peculiar outside. The noise came from the front of the house and sounded like a cry—not of an animal but of a man. She held still while the others filled their plates and then she heard another, louder noise. The room fell silent as the sounds of a scuffle became clear—grunting and a dull thud repeated over and over.

Mandy dropped her napkin onto her chair and dashed to the front door to look out. She cracked it open, and it took a moment for her eyes to adjust to the darkness. In front of the house a man lay on the ground. Everett hovered over him, beating the man with his fists. Even in the pale moonlight she recognized the man on the ground. A scream stung her throat and she jumped back from the door. She turned toward the kitchen table. "It's him! It's Harvey!" Looking back outside, she covered her mouth as she sucked in a breath. A ruckus of chairs scooted in the kitchen, and then footsteps rushed behind her. John gently pushed her away from the door as he and Samuel hurried outside.

Roseanna put her hands on Mandy's shoulders. "Look away, Amanda!"

Mandy ignored her mother's order and stayed there at the door. Her gaze was fixed on Harvey's bloodied face as Everett pounded him into the ground. Samuel and John struggled to get a grip on Everett and pull him away from the man. With his last release of fury, Everett planted his foot firmly into Harvey's throat and left it there. Mandy took one last look at Harvey's motionless body; he was dead.

She staggered back out of the doorway, shocked at what she had witnessed. Roseanna pulled her close in a motherly embrace, but Mandy's arms hung limp at her sides. She heard the men discussing what to do with the body. Then John came into the house and put a hand on her back as he told her mother to take her into the bedroom and barricade the door behind them. He said something about Felix's unknown whereabouts, but Mandy could only hear the sound of her heartbeat thumping in her ears. It matched the rhythm of the pounding blows Everett had delivered to the man who had apparently come to take her again.

Roseanna ushered her into the bedroom as John had instructed. Mandy knelt by the window and peeled back a corner of the gauzy curtain to look out while her mother pushed a small dresser against the closed bedroom door.

"Get away from the window, Amanda."

Mandy ignored her mother's demand. She watched as Everett slipped his hands beneath Harvey's shoulders, lifted the body, and dragged it away. Harvey's head lolled to the side, and Mandy's stomach churned. Her father was following Everett, and she pressed the side of her face against the glass to see them until they went around the house and out of sight.

John walked briskly toward the road. He glanced from side to side as if he expected Felix to attack at any moment. "Mr. Colburn is leaving." She looked back at her mother. "Where is he going?"

"Probably to get Levi." Roseanna knelt on the floor beside Mandy and rubbed her arm. "You shouldn't have watched that. It will give you nightmares."

Mandy thought of the images that had plagued her sleep during the past two months. She shook her head. "No, Mother, I believe it will end my nightmares. I just watched the death of the man who attacked me. I'm not ashamed to admit I feel relieved."

Roseanna picked up the opposite edge of the curtain and looked outside too. "I hope John is able to find Levi quickly. I don't want anyone else getting hurt."

Mandy thought of Everett beating Harvey to death and felt a wicked grin curve her mouth. "If Everett gets a chance to fight Felix, there will be no one left to hurt us."

"Amanda Grace, you shouldn't say such things." Roseanna's parental scold lacked sincerity. "Though I agree it's a relief to know the man who took you is now dead."

"Everett told me he would kill Harvey for what he did to me. I knew his rage was pure, but I didn't imagine he would get the chance to beat Harvey to death."

"They all wanted a chance—the men in our family, the Colburns, probably every man in this village. They all wanted a chance to fight for you... especially Levi." Roseanna let her corner of the curtain fall closed. The moonlight lit half of her face, washing away the creases in her skin. "You should be with him. You and Levi belong together. Do you know you should be with him?"

"Mother," Mandy sighed.

"I'm serious, Amanda. You shouldn't be here, curled up by a window, barricaded in your father's house for safety. You should be in your own home, protected by a husband. Levi loves you and he wants to protect you. He is waiting for you to let him love you. I can see it in the way he watches you. He wants you by his side—and not just in these rare moments of terror—he wants you as his wife."

Mandy started to speak, but her mother gave her arm a squeeze and continued. "You're a beautiful woman and you enjoy the flattering attention men give you, but all the compliments and desirous looks you collect can't compare to the adoration that one man—the right man—would give you in marriage. Beauty fades and, my dear, you may not believe this at twenty-four, but it fades rather quickly. Levi would adore you for the rest of your life if you let him. And to him, your beauty will only increase."

"Mother, years ago I rejected Levi, and it is now the greatest of my many regrets." She rubbed her hand across her forehead and wiped away droplets of sweat that had formed without her knowing it. "My life is situated as it is by my own design. I must live with it. I assure you, my heart aches to have that life with Levi, but …it can't be. And so I have to denounce my longing daily."

Roseanna sighed. "I don't see why."

No, her mother wouldn't know why she couldn't be with Levi, and Mandy planned to keep it that way. She peeled the curtain back again to look out and saw only the grassy front yard and the dark smudge of trees beyond. "How long will we have to wait here?"

"Until your father comes back and tells us it's safe."

Mandy leaned her shoulder against the wall and pulled a curl of hair into her fingers. The silence that spread through the room did little to ameliorate the tension. She imagined Everett and her father handling Harvey's dead body and John at Levi's house telling him what had happened. If Felix had come with Harvey to Good Springs, they were all in danger at the moment, but the men would find him and then it would all be over. But if Harvey had come to the village alone, her freedom wouldn't yet be restored—the overseer and her father and Levi would all demand she remain under guard until the danger was eliminated. She couldn't bear the thought of spending her life locked away. She twined her curl around and around her finger then freed it and started again.

* * *

Levi crouched beside his newly hung bedroom door and screwed a porcelain doorknob into place. Satisfied with the look of the completed hardware in the lamplight, he stood and tested the door's alignment with the strike plate in the doorframe. He closed the door and opened it again, then he looked around the empty room. Mandy had once asked why he would put a door on the bedroom if he planned on living in the house alone. He gathered his tools and picked up the lantern before walking to the kitchen. He set the screwdriver and chisels on the countertop as he thought of the honest answer to her question—he didn't plan to live there alone. He had been determined to leave his father's house—even though tradition stated he should stay and inherit the house and his father's work—but he had never planned to live in his new house alone. He had dreamed of making Mandy his wife. He didn't care if tradition forbade marrying a woman who wasn't a virgin. After a week of thought, he had yet to devise a way to marry her without exposing her past with the traditional vows, but the determination remained.

Levi walked into the front room and set the lantern on the mantel. Scanning the house from that angle, he realized he owned a nearly completed—yet still empty—house. He would soon bring in the new table and chairs that were varnished and drying outside the back door, and he planned to build a new bed, though furniture alone would hardly make the house a home.

The long summer nights had passed, and soon he would light the gray leaf log that waited in the grate. Despite the days spent searching for Mandy and the week spent removing satellite debris from the shore, he had still been able to complete the house before the winter began. Requests for his carpentry work were plentiful and would keep him busy through the cold months ahead.

He reached down to straighten the grate in the fireplace and closed the screen. A faint sound outside made him glance at the back door. It was probably the wind blowing against the varnished furniture that was drying on the porch. He decided to go check on it and walked out of the front room to the short hallway. As he passed the kitchen, the back door flew open. Felix moved through the doorway and lunged at Levi. Levi swung, planting his fist into the side of Felix's face. Before Felix recovered his forward momentum, Levi leveled him with a blow to the gut, forcing the air from his lungs. Felix grunted and dived at him.

Rage engulfed Levi as Felix wrestled him through the hallway and into the front room. He didn't have to think of his mother's death or the robbery on the road or the attack on Mandy and Bethany to motivate his fury. He drew back from Felix and swung, delivering a punch with the intent of killing the malicious intruder. Matched in size and anger, Felix used his strength to try and trap him, but Levi countered every attempt, releasing the fullness of his wrath on Felix for every infraction he and his sons had committed. Felix's age made Levi think it would be a short fight, but Felix was unaffected by his force. They fought with neither man subduing the other until Levi's endurance gave him the upper hand. Felix's breath sounded short and shallow, and Levi drew his fist back when the front door swung open. He assumed it was Harvey coming to join the attack. He spun on his heel ready to hit to the younger of his two enemies but pulled his punch within an inch of John's face. As Levi and John both paused in shock, Felix scurried out the back door and ran toward the forest path.

Levi breathed through his mouth as he looked away from his father. Then he tore through the house and out the back door after Felix. He leapt from the porch and landed on the ground with a thud. The branches of the gray leaf trees rustled unnaturally at the eastern edge of his property. Though he couldn't see Felix, he ran across the yard and onto the forest path, following the sound toward the bluffs. Determined not to let Felix get away, he dodged the low-lying limbs as he hurried down the path. The sound of the nearby ocean grew as he approached the bluffs. It began to muffle the sounds of Felix fleeing ahead. John's voice came from behind Levi, and it obscured the stirring branches and heavy breathing of Felix's flight. Irritation added to Levi's anger. He continued his chase down the forest path until he could no longer hear Felix.

He listened intently but heard only his father's footsteps behind him and the soft and steady hum of the waves breaking in the distance. He rushed to the edge of the forest, where he stopped and scanned the rocky terrain between the forest and the sharp drop of the cliff above the sea. Moonlight enabled him to watch for any movement, any shadow, but he saw no sign of Felix. He felt heavy with the weight of regret and bent forward, resting his hands on his knees. His mind clouded with disbelief. Felix had been in his house within reach and had gotten away. He tasted his disgust and spat on the ground, wishing he had been prepared. He straightened his spine as his father caught up to him.

Blowing out a wordless curse, Levi pushed his hands through his hair. "I thought you were Harvey when you came through the door. That's the only reason I didn't kill him. Now Felix has fled. I had my chance to finish him off and I lost him." He shook his head with disappointment. "I thought you were Harvey."

"I know, son. I came to warn you."

"Warn me? How did you know Felix was coming?"

"Harvey—"

"Is Harvey here too?" He growled the question with such rage John flinched.

"He is dead." John looked from side to side then leaned in. "Harvey approached the Fosters' house a few moments ago. Everett beat him to death in their yard. I was inside with Samuel and Roseanna when Mandy heard the fight. It was over quickly. I didn't ask Everett for his account of the incident, but I am certain his actions were justified."

Levi looked across the bluffs again, his eyes still searching for Felix. He felt a slight sense of relief knowing Harvey was dead—even pride that Everett had delivered justice. But with Felix still out there, he felt defeated. He stepped back and glared at his father. "I had my chance. I wanted Felix dead. I still do, but I lost him."

John looked at the ocean then settled his gaze on Levi. "We only have one enemy left, and there are two of us. We can find him and—"

"And what, Father?" Levi interrupted, perturbed. "Give him a strong rebuke? I'm too disgusted with myself for losing him to be angered by your pacifism. Felix deserves death. He has murdered and he has kidnapped. Even scripture prescribes a sentence of death for those crimes." His tone softened as he spoke, not from calm but from defeat. "It doesn't matter. None of it matters. Go ahead, Father, scold me if you wish. I'm doomed to live with Felix tormenting my village and hurting the women I love and no matter how hard I hit him, he will escape and then return to do it all again."

John didn't reply. Levi waited for it, certain of his father's disappointment. He turned away and looked behind him into the forest, briefly wondering if Felix could have circled back to the village. Though his heart still pounded rapidly, coursing energy through his body, his beaten-down spirit convinced him there was nothing more he could do. As the bleakness of defeat sank in, he covered his face with his hands.

John touched Levi's back. "Look down there, son." His urgent voice was barely above a whisper.

"Where?" Levi pulled his hands away from his face and looked in the direction his father was pointing. John motioned to the south, past the steep, rocky edges of the bluffs where the land sloped to the shore. Levi focused his vision into the dark land and saw the faint outline of an old cabin, untouched since its previous occupant's death.

"Frank's old cabin." John kept his voice quiet. "Felix may have gone inside."

The thought of Felix still being within reach recharged Levi's courage, and with it came a surge of aggressive energy. He tightened his fists and lowered his chin as he stared at the cabin. The creepy shack looked unlivable from a distance. He began to walk with quick, quiet steps along the forest edge and heard his father close behind him. Staying in the shadows as he approached the property in front of the cabin, he tried to remain hidden, hoping to take Felix by surprise if he were hiding inside.

A few sparse trees stood between Levi and the overgrown yard in front the decrepit, one-room shack. He moved behind the wide trunk of an old gray leaf tree then glanced over his shoulder at John and whispered, "The front door is open. Is there a back door?"

"No."

"A window at the back?"

"No, just the one at the front." John sounded out of breath.

Levi lowered his torso and moved behind a boulder to position himself nearer the cabin's decaying front porch. John crouched beside him. "What do you plan to do?"

Levi was too full of renewed hope to entertain his father's justice-quelling rhetoric. He remained silent as he leaned his palms against the cold surface of the weathered stone. Over the sound of the nearby waves, he heard John inhale and anticipated a discouraging speech.

John leaned his head around the boulder. "There is something on the threshold."

Levi glanced at him and then at the entryway of the cabin. "I can't tell what it is from here. I'm going to get closer." He stayed low and moved through the scrub, then he crouched behind a tree trunk near the porch. With a clear view of the darkened doorway, Levi saw the object on the threshold, but not its origin.

John moved in behind him. "It is an overturned boot."

Levi nodded. "I can't tell if it is attached to a body. I need to get closer."

"It could be a trick, son."

"What do you suggest?"

John sat back on his haunches but kept his eyes on the cabin's threshold. "Watch and listen from here before we move in again."

Levi watched the boot in the doorway. He wanted to rush in the cabin swinging but decided if this were another chance at killing Felix, he would be wise to move with focused intent. He wished he had brought a weapon—a bow and arrow, a hunting knife, anything. He glanced at his father beside him and wondered if John would fight too if they were attacked. Levi stared at the boot until his vision blurred. He blinked and looked around the front of the cabin. The rotten porch looked like it would crumble easily.

After plotting his path, Levi stayed low and sneaked to the cabin. He raised his head to the porch railing for a clear view of the doorway. The boot was attached to the leg of a man sprawled on the floor just inside the cabin. Levi snapped his head toward John and motioned for him to come closer. John moved beside him. Levi pointed to the body and looked at his father. John shrugged. Levi watched the body for another moment. He detected no movement, so he stood and saw the long silver and black hair spread across the back of the body.

"It's Felix," Levi whispered to John. "I'm going in."

John made no reply, but he moved beside Levi as they crossed the broken planks of the porch steps. Felix appeared to be dead, but Levi couldn't be certain without touching him. Felix's head was turned to the side and his eyelids were open but unblinking. Levi's pulse pounded as he considered how to ensure the man was dead. He glanced at his father. "Do you think he's dead?"

John lifted a foot and nudged Felix's side. When Felix didn't respond, John shrugged and looked at Levi. Felix's breath had sounded shallow when they had fought in Levi's house. Maybe the man had suffered a heart attack or perhaps lost consciousness from an injury he received in the fight. Levi realized his father would suggest they take him to Lydia for medical care if he were alive. Before he could react to the thought, Felix sucked in a breath and grabbed Levi's ankle. Immediately, John thrust his body between Levi and Felix, dropping his arm into the center of Felix's back. A short choke escaped Felix's throat as his body flattened into the floor, motionless. His grip loosened from Levi's ankle. Levi looked down at his father and swallowed hard. John had plunged a tool through Felix's back and into his heart.

Levi stared down at the insentient criminal on the floor. The last beat of Felix's pierced heart flushed blood across his back. It trickled onto the rotten wood floor and swelled in a shallow pool, mixing with dust and splinters.

Shock coursed through Levi's veins. "Father!" His voice cracked as he stepped away from the body. "You killed him!"

John stood, leaving the handle of the tool protruding from Felix's back. "He was going to try to kill you, son."

"I thought he was already dead." Levi glanced at the body and then at his father. "Is that my chisel?"

"I grabbed it as I ran out of your house." John reached a hand to Levi's shoulder, his fingers trembling. "I didn't want to kill him, son. I had to."

"You saved my life. I wasn't prepared to kill him, but you were." Levi stepped back with short mechanical motions as he considered the possible reactions of the villagers when they found out the overseer had killed a man. He felt responsible and looked his father in the eye. "I will take the blame."

John shook his head. "There should be no guilt in defense, Levi."

"I don't blame you, Father, but some might. You stand in the pulpit every week and preach to the village. This might diminish their respect for you regardless of the cause. I can't allow that."

"I am not ashamed—greatly saddened but not ashamed. I did what needed to be done. I didn't want to, but I had to." John's calm voice was reassuring, though his fingers still trembled.

Levi stared at his enemy's corpse and his gut churned. Mandy would need his strength after what she had witnessed, but he could barely gather the strength to look away from Felix's dead body. He wanted to go to her, to comfort her. She needed him; he had to be strong. He tore his gaze away and looked out the door. "Mandy—"

John raised a shaky hand. "She is fine— barricaded in her bedroom with her mother."

Levi felt a wave of relief. He glanced at the corpse, and the shock of his father's involvement kept his heart pounding hard within his chest. All the anger and bitterness he had felt for eleven years had severed his relationship with his father, and now all he could do was stare at the tool handle protruding from his enemy's dead body. He looked at John and saw the faint lines around his father's eyes and the deep creases across his forehead. Somehow, in that moment his father looked both aged and vital. Levi felt a hard lump rise in his throat and let his words pour out. "I'm so sorry, Father."

"What for?"

"For hating you all these years. I blamed you for Mother's death. I felt like you did nothing to protect her. You weren't prepared then and now I'm the one who wasn't prepared. I hated losing her. I still hate it. I've been so scared I would lose Lydia and Bethany and now Mandy too, so I forced them to stay prepared, yet here I am without a weapon and you defended me. It seems inappropriate to say this while standing over a corpse, but I want to be right with you."

John's expression softened as he gazed at Levi. "I didn't kill him to end your bitterness toward me, but if this has changed your heart, son, I gladly accept it."

CHAPTER TWELVE

L evi spent the evening with his father, Everett, and Samuel moving the corpses to an outbuilding between the chapel and the graveyard in the village. Due to the lateness of the hour and the exhaustion brought by fighting, the men agreed to meet at the cemetery after sunrise to dig the graves. Levi went back to the Colburn house, scrubbed thoroughly, and then fell asleep in the single bed where he had slept his entire life.

A deep sleep settled over Levi as soon as his head met the pillow. He awoke in the morning, in the same position he fell asleep in, to silence—save for the sound of his heartbeat. As he opened his eyes, he noticed the faint light of dawn in the room and remembered the work that awaited him.

He enjoyed the cool morning air as he walked to the graveyard. The first of the fallen leaves swirled in the breeze, confirming autumn's arrival. It gave him a strange twinge of pleasure. He left the cobblestone road and walked across the dewy grass beside the chapel. As he approached the end of the long building, he again felt a sense of pleasurable excitement. Though he reminded himself of the grizzly task he was on his way to perform, the novel feeling of happy anticipation grew.

He wondered if he had lost his mind in the fight, then realized the only thing missing inside him was the ancient yoke of bitterness. His enemies had been defeated. His relationship with his father had been restored. The lack of anger in his soul gave him something he had not fully known since he was twelve years old: joy.

The splintered door to the outbuilding was open. Samuel and Everett were inside the musty shed gathering the tools for grave digging. They met Levi at the door and handed him a shovel. He walked with them to the back of the graveyard where his father stood near the cart loaded with two wrapped bodies. Felix and Harvey would be buried beside Christopher's grave. In the two months since his burial, the ground over Christopher's grave had already started to settle back into place.

Connor and Lydia met them at the gravesite. As the village physician, Lydia's confirmation of death was required before the bodies could be buried. She gave a quick check of each body and confirmed their deaths. Levi was usually amazed at his sister's impassive demeanor in such circumstances, but she fanned her face and pressed her hand against her stomach, seeming particularly unsettled.

Levi worked to keep his newfound enthusiasm to himself as Lydia gave her professional permission to bury the bodies. Though the previous night's experience had given him a sense of soul-freeing satisfaction, its outward manifestation would be inappropriate at present. Connor put his hand to the small of Lydia's back and began to walk her home. Levi imagined them in ten years—Connor with gray at his temples and Lydia carrying one child on her hip and three more running around them.

John moved along the edge of Christopher's grave. With his shovel, he scratched a rectangle in the sandy soil marking two feet wide and six feet long. Then he walked along the edge of that rectangle and scratched another mark for a second grave. Everett and Samuel began digging one grave, while Levi and his father dug the other. They removed the upper grass from the earth and dug without stopping until the holes were about four feet deep. The men laid a body in each grave on the bare ground and then shoveled dirt from the nearby piles to fill the holes. They stabbed a wooden marker—inscribed with the deceased's name and date of death—into the sod at the head of each grave.

John breathed through his mouth from exhaustion and nodded to the other men when the work was complete. Levi returned the shovels to the outbuilding, then he glanced at the road and saw Everett pulling the empty cart as he and Samuel returned to their farm.

Levi removed his work gloves as he stepped through the wet grass. John came alongside him and they walked together past the chapel, across the cobblestones, and down the road to the Colburn property. Neither said a word, and the comfortable silence brought Levi assurance in the complete forgiveness between them.

* * *

Sunlight spilled through the narrow windows and into the crowded chapel. Mandy turned sideways as she shuffled between the pews and sat beside Lydia. Since Harvey and Felix were dead—though Mandy didn't know the details of Felix's death—she expected the Sunday service to have a different tone than usual as John Colburn stepped to the pulpit.

Mandy heard the muted scuff of feet on the wooden floor as the last congregants found seats. A woman in the pew in front of Mandy fussed over a child's Sunday dress. It reminded her of her mother's behavior when she was a little girl. The thought made her smile.

Levi stepped into the row and sat between Mandy and the end of the wooden pew. She had not seen him since the night they argued in the shed. She wondered if he had let it go, or if it had ignited old resentments. He sat close to her and folded his hands in his lap. Mandy noticed the two-day-old cuts across his knuckles. His face was freshly shaven, and his shirt collar was ironed to a crisp blue peak. He glanced at her and gave a small smile, then he turned his attention to the front of the chapel as his father began his weekly sermon.

John Colburn prayed and then kept his head bowed for a moment, somber and silent. Mandy felt Levi's arm slip over the back of the pew behind her. She accepted his gesture with the hope of a mutual reprieve. His fingers curled around her shoulder and she instinctively leaned into his side. She imagined being his wife and sitting in church with their children beside them. Though it could never be, the yearning remained despite her effort to ignore it.

John looked out at the congregation. "Felix Colburn, a descendent of my own ancestry, came with his son to attack our village Friday evening. These men have caused great destruction in our lives over the course of many years. Their offenses include causing the death of my wife, robbing my son, the recent attack on one of my daughters, and the violent abduction of a beloved village daughter." John's gaze landed on Mandy briefly and quickly moved to others in the crowd. "We have heard various accounts of their savage attacks in other villages over the years as well. They came into our village with a destructive plan, but men of Good Springs thwarted that plan. Felix Colburn and his sons, Harvey and Christopher, lived by the sword and—just as the scripture warns—they also perished by the sword. It is with a heavy but relieved heart I report to you these men are no longer a threat to our village or the Land. Their bodies have been laid to rest among our departed loved ones as a testimony of our forgiveness. We forgive because we have been forgiven. Don't pronounce judgment on them, people of Good Springs, when you pass by their graves, assuming by their sinful lives that they are receiving eternal punishment, for the God who saves us promises to save all who call upon his name. We shouldn't presume to know a man's final thoughts, and in our forgiven hearts we should hope these men called upon God. If they did—just like the one repentant thief crucified beside Jesus—they are now present with the Lord in glory. May that give you hope for the souls of the departed; however, let it not be an excuse for your own choices."

As Mandy absorbed the overseer's gracious words, she felt Levi's warmth. She tried to direct her attention to the pulpit but could think only of the man beside her. She felt the slow rise and fall of his side with each breath. He kept his arm around her for the remainder of the service, and she hoped his gesture meant more than the comfort of a friend.

She glanced at Lydia beside her, wanting to glean a look acknowledging Levi's gesture, but Lydia sat with her eyes fixed on the overseer. Mandy grinned at her friend; Lydia was always perfectly attentive in church.

When the sermon ended, Levi gave her shoulder a squeeze as he left the pew. She assumed he went back to open the chapel doors. She glanced through the rows of rising congregants to the back of the chapel but couldn't see him. As she stood to leave, she got caught in conversation with other villagers. Though she tried to focus her attention on their pleasantries, her gaze repeatedly moved toward the chapel's open doors.

Roseanna passed her in the aisle. "Amanda, I have a roast in the oven and I need to see Mrs. Ashton home. Will you tend to it for me?"

"Yes, Mother." Mandy excused herself from conversation and made her way out of the church. She descended the chapel steps and moved around a small crowd. As her feet touched the cobblestone street, she heard Levi's voice behind her. She glanced over her shoulder and stopped walking as he hurried to her. He had a tiny yellow daisy pinched between his forefinger and thumb.

Levi looked genuinely happy as he came beside her. "May I walk you home?"

Mandy smiled. She wanted to be with him not for protection, but because she loved him. She studied him and inclined her head. "The danger has passed, so I no longer need an escort."

"That's right." His grin didn't waver. He held out the little flower to her. "May I walk you home?"

"Yes." She chuckled and took the flower and began to walk beside him. At the edge of the village, the cobblestones ended and the road became gravel. The pebbles crunched beneath their feet in a slow rhythm. She took his arm even though it had not been offered.

He glanced down at her hand on his arm and looked her in the eye. "As you said, the danger has passed."

Her natural tendency to flirt tempted her lashes to flutter. No matter her growing desire for a life with him, she had to protect her family's honor. She drew a breath and repeated his words. "That's right."

He smiled as he put his hand on top of hers and smoothed her fingers around his arm. He seemed to be exuding an uncommon happiness, and it piqued her curiosity. She held up her hand to block the sun from her eyes and glanced at him. "Is it the return of safety in the village that has caused your happiness?"

"Sure—at least partially." He looked at her, still grinning, and then at the road ahead. "I feel like a new man." His calloused fingers moved across the skin of her hand. She studied the healing marks along his knuckles. Everett's hands looked the same way from fighting Harvey.

Though no one else was on the road, she lowered her voice. "Everett is also happy. It seems strange after having killed a man."

His eyebrows raised then lowered, but his gaze stayed on the road ahead. "I didn't kill anyone."

"I meant in defense, of course... ending the life of an evil man."

"I didn't end anyone's life."

His words mystified her. She had been certain he killed Felix. She glanced up at the gray leaf tree limbs arching overhead. The silvery leaves of the trees met halfway over the road and intertwined in a thick blend that blocked the sun. She sighed. "I thought your father said that Felix is dead."

"He is." Levi put both of his hands in his pockets. "I can't say any more about what happened. Perhaps I will be able to tell you one day but not yet."

She kept her hand around his arm. She didn't understand what he meant, but she trusted him. They walked in silence along the road. Then, when she couldn't bear her curiosity any longer, she glanced at him again. "What has caused the other part?"

He turned only his eyes toward her. "Of what?"

"You said that securing our safety was only part of the reason for your happiness. I wondered what the other part was."

"Oh." He nodded and drew a breath. "I made peace with my father. I finally came to an understanding of the things that used to anger me. I didn't want to be that man anymore. I let go of the demands and bitterness and found forgiveness. It's really freeing." He removed a hand from his pocket and tapped his chest. "I feel like I have more room to breathe."

As Levi spoke of his liberation, Mandy studied his joyful demeanor. It was refreshing to see him happy. She thought of moments of forgiveness and release in her life and smiled. "I'm pleased to hear it—for you and for your father. How did he react to your confession?"

"He was quick to forgive. I always thought my father's graciousness was a pretense—a part of his profession—and I wanted nothing to do with it." He grinned. "Do you know that feeling on a cloudy day when just before dusk the clouds break directly overhead and it casts an unnatural light on everything?" She nodded and he continued. "That's how I feel with my father now. I held such dark opinions of him and couldn't understand why everyone else seemed blind to his nature. Now I know the animosity I felt wasn't between us—it was in me." He looked serious for a moment and then shook his head. "I misspent many years harboring resentment, but no more."

"It seems we all have some reason to be bitter, but since we have life before us, we also have a reason to let it go." Mandy glanced at the pasture as they approached her family's property. She had not set foot on that pasture since the day she was hauled across it against her will. The barn in the distance caught her attention. She felt the urge to be in her workshop creating the instruments that gave meaning to her emptiness, but she didn't want to part ways with Levi again and leave anything unsaid. "I'm sorry about the other night. I hated fighting with you, and I was wrong."

"Don't worry about it."

She slowed their pace as they walked onto her family's property. "No, I need to say this. You asked me if there was something more between us. I wasn't prepared for that and I handled it poorly. The truth is… you mean a lot to me. Not only because you rescued me and protected me, but also because you listened to me, and you didn't judge me. I know I can trust you always. And you were right: we are different together now. It probably sounds bizarre, but I'm grateful for what happened to me because I came out of it with your friendship. That's how much you mean to me." Her face felt hot as if she were blushing. "I'm not telling you this to stir intrigue—we both know there can be nothing more because of my past and the village's tradition—but you deserve to know that I like being with you."

Mandy let go of Levi's arm and he caught her hand in his. He held it and looked at her. His eyes were serious, but he had not lost his grin. The sun's rays touched his face and golden specks lit the brown of his eyes. He seemed to be asking something with a look, but she didn't know what. She glanced at the farmhouse and back at him. "Would you like to join us for dinner?"

He shook his head and then let go of her hand. "Thank you, but there is something I must finish."

"Well, thank you for walking me home."

When Levi simply smiled, Mandy nodded and turned and walked to her house. Shep hobbled down from the porch and bounded toward her, tail wagging.

She glanced back once and saw Levi walking across the road to his property.

* * *

Mandy wiped a clean rag over the polished surface of a newly completed violin and dropped the cloth onto her workbench. She plucked the violin's strings and adjusted the tuning, then she raised the new wood instrument to her chin. Delight flushed through her as she moved the bow across the violin for the first time.

After Mandy played a few scales, she began to play the melody of an old hymn her grandfather had taught her when she was a child. It was the first song she played on each instrument she crafted, though her reason for the ritual escaped her. She never sang the hymn while she played, but she always meditated on the lyrics as each note rang out. The hymn called for praise and spoke of redemption and the triumph of grace. Mandy understood those themes more now than ever. She thought of Levi's recent reconciliation with his father and his evident peace when he told her about it on their walk home only days before.

As she began the last stanza of the hymn, Mandy glanced at the open door and saw John Colburn leaning against the doorframe, watching her play. With his arms crossed over his chest and his head slightly tilted, the overseer reminded her of Levi.

She smiled at him and lowered the bow to her side. "Hello, Mr. Colburn."

"Please, don't stop on my account. That is one of my favorite hymns." He began to hum the melody as he stepped into the workshop. "I was downstairs helping your father and heard you playing. I hoped you wouldn't mind my visit."

"Not at all." She gestured to the wooden stool in front of her workbench, offering it to John, but he shook his head.

He motioned for her to sit instead. Then he scratched his trimmed beard. "I wondered how you are coping with everything that happened last week."

"Fine, I'm sure." Mandy answered quickly as she sat on the wooden stool. She set the violin and bow on her workbench and looked up at the overseer. John leaned a hand on the surface of the workbench and waited for her to elaborate. His intense gaze made her feel small—not insignificant but childlike—and forced her to ponder his question further. "Felix and Harvey's deaths brought an end to my nightmare—everyone else's too, I suppose. I will probably struggle for years to come with the memory of being attacked, but I'm ready to move forward."

John nodded and pursed his lips. "Your father tells me you won't be performing next week. It would be quite a disappointment to the village if you didn't contribute your beautiful music to your father's annual party. It would hardly seem like autumn in Good Springs without dancing in the Fosters' barn."

"Mr. Colburn..." Mandy looked down at her hands and began to pick at her varnish-stained cuticles. "I mean no disrespect by refusing to perform. On the contrary, my purpose is to avoid drawing attention to myself. There are other musicians who will play."

She heard John's deep exhalation and glanced at him. He nodded as if he understood, but she looked away, thinking he couldn't possibly understand her motivation.

"Amanda, I believe returning to your old routine—not old behavior but your usual activities—will cultivate the sense of normalcy you desire." He lifted a hand and smiled. "But I didn't come up here to persuade you to perform at the party. When I heard you playing, I felt I should encourage you to use your gift for the good of the community. Your music is important to this village. You are important to this village and to my family... particularly to my son."

Mandy's eyes shot up to him and—when he smiled—she realized she had just given her thoughts away.

John walked past her and examined some of the unfinished instruments in their various stages of completion on shelves along the opposite wall. "Sometimes you remind me of Hannah; the resemblance isn't physical but in spirit. I often wonder if Levi realizes it. Do you remember much about Mrs. Colburn?" When John glanced at Mandy, she smiled and shook her head.

He tapped a finger on a carved violin piece and continued speaking as he inspected the instruments. "Hannah was creative... contemplative... playful... occasionally mischievous. She was musical, too. She was always singing or humming. When I asked for her hand in marriage, she was barely eighteen, yet she carried herself with such dignity. Years later, when I stepped into my father's position, she filled her role as an overseer's wife quite gracefully. At home, she had a fiery wit and aired unorthodox opinions that others were rarely privy to. I found her mysterious and lighthearted at the same time. She was respectful and refreshing, though I never felt like I knew her fully. At first her complexity confused me, but as our love grew, it enticed me all the more. I made it my life's ambition to study her." John looked at a shelf of tools as he spoke. "I see that passion in Levi's devotion to you."

Mandy felt her jaw drop open and she promptly closed it. Levi had made his attraction to her obvious in the past, but the thought of him presently being passionately devoted to her came as a surprise. She decided the overseer had not been as astute in his observations as she previously credited him. Still, the sweetness of being loved the way John described loving his late wife made Mandy wish he were right about Levi.

John turned back from the shelf and looked at her. "So you will consider it then?"

"Pardon?"

"Will you consider performing at your father's party?"

"Oh, yes." Mandy chuckled and felt heat in her face. "Of course, Mr. Colburn, I will consider it."

* * *

Levi stood on the front porch of his house, examining the wood grain on the new double bed he had built from leftover gray leaf lumber. The sound of wagon wheels diverted his attention to the road. Samuel Foster directed a team of horses as they pulled his wagon onto Levi's property and close to his house. Fallen leaves crunched under the wagon's wheels as it rolled to a stop. Everett jumped from the back of the wagon and grinned when his feet hit the ground. "We have something for you, Levi."

Levi descended the porch steps and walked to Samuel. "What is all this?"

Samuel looped the reins around the wagon bench, then he set the brake and climbed down with a grunt. "It's a cook stove for your new kitchen, my boy!"

Levi put his hand on the wagon's side and looked at the new, lacquered stove. Everett let down the gate at the back of the wagon and pulled a length of stovepipe into his arms. As Everett carried the pipe into the house, Samuel patted Levi's shoulder. "This is the least I can do."

Levi looked at him. "I don't understand. You owe me nothing, Mr. Foster."

"Oh, but I do." His chin quivered under his white beard until he pressed his lips together. "You brought my daughter home. She was taken from us—ripped from our lives—and you found her. The day you brought her home, I asked Roseanna what we could possibly do for you and she said you would need a stove in your new house. So I sent trade to the iron man in Southpoint right away." He motioned to the stove on the wagon. "I had hoped it would arrive before you completed the house, but you're a fast builder. The trader assured me it would fit through the front door."

"Thank you. I'm overwhelmed." Levi glanced at Everett as he came out of the house and returned to the wagon. Everett picked up another length of pipe and several tools. Levi noticed Everett's cheeky grin and knew he had some secret that he hoped would be discovered.

As Everett took the tools into the house, Samuel inched closer to Levi. "There is one more thing. Years ago you asked for my blessing with Mandy and I gladly gave it. You weren't the only person disappointed when she rejected you. She was very young, very foolish then, you understand? But I'm a man who truly believes our past is best left behind us. I want you to know you still have my blessing, son, should you ever need it."

Levi began to reply, but Samuel glanced at the house and held up a finger. Levi looked back and saw Everett walking down the porch steps, still wearing his goofy grin. Despite Samuel's attempt to conceal the matter, Everett was obviously aware of his father's purpose. Samuel turned to the wagon and cleared his throat. "When we find ourselves given a second chance, we should all be sure to use it wisely."

CHAPTER THIRTEEN

Mandy perched on the edge of the round, cushioned seat in front of her dressing table and tried not to wrinkle the back of her new dress. With a row of hairpins trapped between her lips, she swirled her long curls behind her head, twisting the hunk of hair upon itself again and again until the bulk of it was subdued in a tight knot at the nape of her neck. She plucked the hairpins from her lips one at a time and secured the wiry bun into place. The stubborn shorter curls along her hairline broke free from the bun and framed her face without permission. She glanced in the mirror one last time and smoothed her eyebrows into fine arches before she left her bedroom.

As Mandy walked into the kitchen, her mother marched out of the linen closet carrying a tall stack of folded napkins. "It takes a whole day just to wash and iron these after the party each year, but it's worth it."

Mandy opened her hands. "I can take them outside."

"Thank you. Don't you look lovely! You should get a shawl—there's already a chill in the air."

Roseanna unloaded the stack into Mandy's arms. "Everett is lighting the lanterns in the barn."

"He needs to tune his guitar before people start arriving." Mandy pushed the back door open with her elbow. "The wagons will be pulling up any minute. Are you coming?"

"I have to get my dancing shoes. I'll be right out." Roseanna winked then disappeared down the hallway.

As Mandy stepped out the door, she propped her chin on top of the napkins to steady the stack. She moved carefully through the yard and stopped at one of the picnic tables in front of the barn. After she set the napkins down, she divided them into smaller stacks. Then she smoothed the ribbing at the front of her gray dress and wished she could spend the evening in her workshop instead of performing.

Everett jogged out of the barn and brushed dust from the dark buttoned vest he wore over a dress shirt. As he unrolled his sleeves, he stopped in front of Mandy. "Are you ready to start the music?"

"Not really. This is my first time in front of a crowd since..." She looked at the setting sun, then back at Everett as she wiped her sweaty palms on her dress. "I don't want to draw attention to myself."

"I know." He gave her a look that was more paternal than that of a younger sibling. "You'll be fine. The village needs this. We all do." A wagon pulled in from the road and he turned his head. "Would you tune my guitar for me, please? Father is preparing the roast, and I have to direct the wagons."

"Of course."

Everett buttoned his sleeves at the wrist as he started toward the incoming wagon. Mandy watched him meet guests at the entrance. The back of the open wagon was filled with children singing. Another wagon turned in behind the first. Most of the villagers would be on the property before the sun went down, and they would be ready to dance.

Mandy walked through the wide doorway and into the empty barn. The floor had been swept clean, and wooden benches lined the walls. Dozens of lanterns hung from the rafters. She stepped to the center of the room where the instruments were set up on a small platform. She had added several extra instruments for the village's musicians who would take a turn performing. First she tuned the violins, then the guitars. She carried a crate of gourd shakers to the door for the village children to play with. As she walked back to the center of the barn, people began filing into the spacious open building. They were smiling and anticipating a song. Mandy picked up her grandfather's old violin. She felt a slight tremble in her fingertips but willed herself to focus on the music. Remembering the overseer's encouragement to use her gift to bless the village, she smiled at the children entering the barn and started to play.

Wagon after wagon arrived. Some people came into the barn and began to dance; others milled around the tables outside. At dusk Mandy saw Everett lighting lanterns on the tables outside. It was time to eat. The final note resounded from her violin and she lowered her bow to her side. After carefully placing the old violin back in its case, she went outside and surveyed the crowd.

Two little girls followed her and latched onto her hands. As she told them how beautiful they were in their dancing skirts, she glanced up and saw Levi walking his elderly aunt to a table. The girls pulled at Mandy's arms, both asking her questions at the same time, but her eyes remained fixed on Levi. She watched as he helped Isabella to her seat, then he carefully draped her shawl over her shoulders. Isabella said something to him and he laughed with her before he stepped away. As Mandy watched him, she thought of how he took care of his family, of his gentleness, and of his strength. He looked up at Mandy and stopped walking as if the sight of her surprised him somehow. His mouth slowly curved in half a smile and she wondered what he was thinking. The girls hanging from her arms both raised their volume, begging for her attention. She forced herself to remove her gaze from Levi and looked down at the girls to answer their question. "Yes, girls, I would love to sit by you."

Roseanna whirled by Mandy and handed her an apron. "I need you in the serving line, Amanda. One of my helpers stood too close to the roasting fire and got the vapors. I sent her into the house to lie down." Roseanna waved a hand at the girls. "Go sit with your mother, girls. Miss Foster is busy."

Mandy shrugged at the frowning children and then followed Roseanna to the serving line. She glanced back at Levi, but the crowd had moved, obstructing her view of him.

Mandy tied on the apron and stood behind the food table with the hired helpers. She smiled as she spooned beans onto every plate held in front of her. The usual compliments on her appearance flowed from the mouths of the well-meaning villagers. She replied with humble thanks but inwardly wished to hear something besides a comment on her appearance.

As the end of the line drew near, Mandy felt her nervousness for the coming performance return. She scraped the inside of the bean pot with the serving spoon and looked at the last few guests who were waiting for food. Everett followed Bethany in line. Mandy watched how her brother stood close behind Bethany. Though they were still young, they were no longer the animated and comedic pair they once were. They leaned into each other as they spoke, as if their shared observations were now private matters. Everett kept his face close to Bethany's hair as he waited behind her. Mandy wondered if Bethany knew she was adored and if the adoration were mutual.

The line of guests continued to pass in front of Mandy. Connor held both his plate and Lydia's as they walked by. Lydia's hand covered her stomach. While Mandy spooned food onto the plates, she noticed Lydia's sour expression. "Lydia, are you well?"

Lydia nodded and looked away. Connor grinned and wiggled his eyebrows at Mandy as they kept walking.

Levi was the last person in the line. He held out an empty plate as he stepped in front of Mandy. "You're working hard tonight."

She noticed he didn't comment on her dress or her hair, and for that she was grateful. She smiled. "It's my pleasure." She lifted the spoon to scoop food onto his plate but stopped short. "Wait—you don't like beans."

Levi grinned. "Yes, that's true."

Mandy withdrew the serving spoon and let it hover over the pot. She chuckled at him. "Then why would you accept a heaping spoonful?"

"I will take anything you offer."

Mandy grinned—thinking of food—but when she caught Levi's gentle and unwavering stare, she detected deeper meaning and felt her smile fade. His gaze remained fixed on her and she wondered if this was a glimpse of the passionate devotion that John had mentioned. Or maybe Levi was simply being polite while he waited for her response and she stood mouth agape and wordless. She willed herself to say something—anything—but could produce no sound as her thoughts congealed.

Roseanna breezed behind her. "Time to get back in there, Amanda. They'll be ready for music soon, and I want to dance. Hello, Levi."

Levi grinned and moved along to the other helpers waiting to serve the last guest. Mandy set the spoon into the dwindling bean pot then untied the apron, rolled it into a quick ball, and dropped it on the table. She took a pastry from a basket at the end of the table and picked at it on her way back into the barn.

As she ambled to the small platform in the center of the barn floor, Mandy wondered what had come over her when she saw Levi. The notion of devoted love from the one man who truly knew her had stirred her desire for the impossible. Though she told herself not to entertain such a hurtful longing, images of proof of Levi's devotion streamed through her mind. Mandy shook her head as an outward effort to stop the inward distraction, and she picked up one of the new wood violins to check its tuning.

The drummer tapped his sticks together while a few eager guests waited on the floor in front of the stage. Everett darted through the entrance and straight to his guitar. He pulled its strap over his shoulder and looked at Mandy for her cue. She raised her bow and filled the expansive barn with jubilant sound. Skirts twirled and feet stomped as most of the villagers flowed into the barn. Mandy scanned the familiar faces in the crowd. Many of the men tried to hold her gaze, but she never let her eyes settle on anyone. The tunes varied in style and tempo. Between songs, dancers changed partners and shawls piled on the wooden benches. The barn quickly warmed from the crowd's heat.

Mandy noticed Levi standing near the doorway. A young lady in a lavender dress stood in front of him. She had her arms crossed behind her back, and she smiled and swayed to the music as she talked to Levi. When he laughed at whatever the young woman said, Mandy felt an unpleasant surge of jealousy. She averted her eyes, but the burning visceral ache remained.

When the song ended, Mandy glanced back and saw the young woman was still close to Levi as if she were waiting for him to ask her to dance. Mandy had planned to perform the waltz next but—knowing what Levi would and wouldn't dance to—she chose instead to play a jig. She directed her eyes to the dancers nearest the platform and condemned herself for her envious spirit. When she looked again, Levi was gone.

After the jig, Everett leaned close to Mandy. "Time to slow it down." She nodded, then she took a breath and closed her eyes, willing herself to focus only on the music. Drawing the bow across the strings, she began the waltz and let each note ring out in the slow three-four rhythm. The emptiness inside the hollow cavity of the violin resonated with the ache in her heart.

* * *

Relief washed over Levi when Mrs. Ashton finally waved her granddaughter back to her. Levi was the only person the young lady had been introduced to, so he had made polite conversation. But by the way the girl smiled and swished her dress, he realized she wanted him to ask her to dance. And since he had no intention of focusing on anyone but Mandy, he removed himself from his position as soon as the young lady was called away to her grandmother.

Levi thrust his hands into his pockets and meandered around the outskirts of the crowd in the barn. He had known of the possibility that Mandy wouldn't perform, and it pleased him to see her gracing the village with her gift. Her decision was indicative of healing, and that was what he most wanted for her. She appeared confident and controlled, though different in her performance than she used to be. She was less interested in captivating the audience and more entranced by the music.

When Mandy began to play the waltz, Levi expected Connor to take Lydia to the dance floor as he had both previous years. When they remained stationary in the crowd, Levi moved toward them, concerned. Lydia looked flushed. She fanned her face with her hands. "It's so stuffy in here. I'm going outside to get some fresh air."

Levi watched her walk to the door and turned to Connor. "Is she all right?"

"Yeah, she's okay." Connor looked back at the stage.

Levi nodded. No matter Lydia's reason, she was right—it was stuffy in the crowded barn. He stepped back from the rest of the people who were watching the dancers and found an empty place along the back wall where he could see Mandy. He watched her face as she played. Her eyes were closed. The distance was too great to see the details of her features clearly, but he knew her lashes fluttered when she closed her eyes and played. He heard a clarity and length to the notes of the old, familiar tune as she performed. Her music flowed through the air in an unhurried resonance, fueled by emotion and experience.

Levi noticed Everett standing at the back of the stage with his guitar strapped over his shoulder. He was craning his neck to watch the dancers. Levi spotted Bethany dancing with a boy from her class then understood Everett's interest. Bethany's last year of schooling had begun, and Levi wondered if Everett would be waiting at their doorstep, flowers in hand, as soon as the year was over.

When the song ended, the crowd applauded and the dancers dispersed. Mandy stepped back from the front of the stage and motioned for another player to take her place. As the other musicians began a song in full rhythmic pulses, Mandy slipped through the crowd and up the stairs to the loft. Levi couldn't see the door to her workshop from where he stood on the barn floor, but he knew where she went. His confidence soared. He knew what she needed and—this time—he was prepared.

* * *

Levi curled his forefinger and used his knuckle to knock on the door to Mandy's workshop. While he waited for her to answer, he glanced over the loft's railing and down at the stage on the barn floor below. Everett looked up at him and nodded, acknowledging his cue. Levi's knee quivered, so he shifted his weight to the other foot. The door cracked open and Mandy peeked out. Her somber, green eyes warmed quickly when they met his. "Levi." Her expression immediately changed, and it pleased him.

He inclined his head to match the angle of hers. "May I come in?"

"Of course." She stepped back and pulled the door open. "Do they need me downstairs?"

"No." He walked into the dimly lit room and lifted his hand to the lantern on her workbench. Wanting to glean every possible clue from her aspect, he turned the knob on the lantern and increased its flame.

Mandy closed the door, muffling the sounds from the party below. She walked past him and sat on a wooden stool in front of her workbench. She pulled pins from her hair and dropped them on the workbench next to the lantern, one hairpin at a time. With her eyes fixed on the growing pile of pins, she let out a heavy sigh. "I had to get away. I can't explain it."

"You don't have to explain yourself to me."

"I probably seemed rude—it's my family's party—but I couldn't perform any longer."

"You weren't rude at all. You worked hard tonight." Levi watched her hair fall behind her shoulders as she set it free. He stepped close enough to touch her but forced himself to wait. "I came up here to talk to you about something—something important—but if you are tired, I can wait."

"I'm fine, really." Mandy sat up straight as if to prove her alertness. A curl dropped over her cheek.

With one finger, Levi pushed the hair off her face. She didn't flinch at his touch, but her eyes darted to meet his. The full sound of the gray leaf guitar began to swell downstairs, and he was grateful for Everett's good timing. "Do you know this song?"

Mandy gave a small nod. "I haven't heard it in years."

"That's why I asked Everett to play it. This is the song that was playing all those years ago when I asked to court you." He watched her eyes, ready to take in even the slightest signal.

"Oh." She pressed her lips together and nodded. "I'm sorry. I didn't remember that this was the song."

He shrugged. "That night didn't affect you the way it did me."

Her thin eyebrows drew together. "Levi, you should know that decision is one of my deepest regrets. Actually, it has become the deepest regret of my life." A smile escaped Levi's control and she nodded. "I see that brings you satisfaction."

"Yes, please forgive me but it does." He reached for her hands and she stood as he slowly stepped back. "Dance with me."

Mandy moved into a formal stance but, ignoring tradition, Levi slid his hand behind her back and pulled her close. As the music drifted up into the workshop, he danced her gently across the dusty floor. Their feet moved in unhurried rhythm. He brought their joined hands to his chest. She rested her head against his collar. In the lantern light, they cast a single shadow across a row of half-completed instruments.

Their feet stilled before the song ended. Levi loosened his grip but didn't let go. Mandy pulled back and looked up at him. He studied her face and found the kind of intimacy expected between old friends but no indication of the kind of attraction reserved for passion. He felt the quiver again in his knees. The risk of rejection was as great now as it was the last time he laid his heart at her feet.

She seemed to sense his nervousness. Her lips curved in a slight grin. "Are you going to ask me to court?"

"No." Disappointment flashed across her face, and it encouraged him. "I don't see the point in courting. I already know everything I need to know about you. I have watched you grow and change. You have proven you no longer favor the distant admiration of many men. But tell me: do you still wish to forgo the deep affections of one man?"

Her eyes softened, confirming her understanding of the moment. When she didn't answer, he continued. "I'm not here to ask you to court but to marry. I have loved you my entire life thus far, and I will continue to love you for the remainder of my days whether you love me or not. But if you do love me, Amanda Foster, say it and I will marry you."

A smile bowed the edges of Mandy's mouth and her eyes brightened. Her voice was barely above a whisper. "I do love you, Levi."

"Marry me."

"I will."

He released his held breath and felt a surge of elation. He leaned down and kissed her. When he pulled away, he watched her eyes flutter open. She smiled first, then she looked down and her face changed.

"What is it?"

Mandy's hands slowly dropped to her sides. "Levi, you know about my past but my family does not. By the traditional vows, my father will have to testify I'm a spotless bride. I can't let him do that, nor can I bear to disappoint him with the truth. I don't care what the village thinks of me, but I won't shame my family."

He lifted her chin with a finger. "I have already taken care of it."

"What do you mean?"

"Since I broke from tradition by choosing my own profession and building my own home, neither of our fathers was surprised when I told them I wanted our wedding to diverge from tradition. The only vows in our wedding will be between you and me."

Mandy looked astonished and lifted her hands to his chest. "You kept my secret."

"Yes." He covered her hands with his. "Next Saturday—one week from tomorrow—leave your father's house and meet me at the chapel at noon. I will vow to love you faithfully all of my days. Then I will take you home with me to the house I have built for us."

"One week?" Mandy beamed. "So you are going to keep the tradition of Preparation Week. Does the village know?"

He glanced at the closed door and back at Mandy. The music had stopped and it was quiet in the barn below. She pointed at the door. "Are they waiting for my answer?"

"Only our families. Everett is waiting for my signal whether or not to announce it to the village."

Mandy let out a small laugh and put her hand over her mouth. "What is your signal?"

Levi stepped to the door. "Whether or not I walk out alone."

CHAPTER FOURTEEN

Mandy folded a set of finely embroidered muslin curtains, hugged them to her chest, and smiled at Lydia. "Thank you. They are really beautiful."

"It's just my part in the preparations." Lydia sighed and sat at the desk in her medical office. "Levi will take them to the house later today and hang them. He probably won't be pleased I showed you first, but I wanted to make sure you liked the design."

Mandy set the folded curtains on the corner of Lydia's desk and lowered herself into the chair beside it. "I can't imagine the amount of work he's done this week to get the house ready by Saturday. Not just him—the whole village. It's all a bit overwhelming."

Lydia propped her elbows on the desk. "How much of the preparations have you seen?"

"Well, I haven't seen the house this week, of course. Bethany showed me the dishes she made at the pottery and I've noticed the parade of villagers going to Levi's house—"

"Your house," Lydia corrected.

"Our house." Mandy pressed her fingers to her temples and shook her head. "I still can't believe it."

"In two short days you will be a Colburn."

"We will be sisters." Mandy giggled. "Did you ever think that would happen?"

"No… yes… no, but I'm thrilled with the way things turned out—for you and for Levi. I'm sure you both will be very happy together. Is your dress ready yet?"

Mandy nodded. "Mother brought it home yesterday. The color is a lovely light blue. I liked the white dress you wore when you married Connor, but you've not worn it since."

"I thought it was an impractical color, but I wore white for Connor's sake. He said it's the tradition in his land for the bride to wear a white dress. They believe it symbolizes the bride's purity."

"Oh, well, I'm relieved we have no such tradition."

Lydia wrinkled her nose and waved her hand as if shooing away the notion. "He said most brides there wear white even though few of them are actually pure."

"Yet here the brides are rarely blemished." Regretful, Mandy looked down at her hands. Levi had promised never to speak of her past. He was willing to give up his honor for her mistake, and to her that would forever be proof of his love. She lifted her head. "Levi said in our wedding ceremony he and I will say our vows, but there will be none of the other traditions."

Lydia's eyes widened then she nodded. "I wasn't sure how he would do it, but I knew he would find a way to protect you. A simpler ceremony seems perfect for the two of you."

"Do you think people will wonder about me since we are breaking from tradition?"

"No, especially since Levi has our father's support. Besides, once you're pronounced Levi's lawfully wedded wife, no one will have the right to question your past."

Mandy sighed and looked at the ceiling then back at Lydia. "It is befitting of Levi."

"It is redemptive. He's truly devoted to you."

"And I plan to give him a life worthy of such devotion."

When someone knocked lightly on the door, Lydia stood to answer it. As she walked to the door, she put a hand over her abdomen. She rubbed her flat belly while she whispered to the person at the door. "I'm not with a patient but your bride is in here, so you will have to come back later."

Mandy heard the quiet murmurings of Levi's low voice and felt desperate to see him. In keeping with the tradition, they had not spoken since the night of the betrothal. One week apart to prepare for their union seemed like an eternity. Knowing she would spend her life with Levi did little to ease her constant desire to be with him. The week had given her nervous anticipation that fluxed from quiet desperation to giddy eagerness.

Lydia closed the door and stepped back to her desk grinning. "I have a message for you, but I'm not sure if that is allowed."

Mandy craved any word from Levi. She scooted to the edge of her seat. "Would you torment your dearest friend?"

"Perhaps." Lydia smirked. "Levi said he loves you—that is all I will relay."

Mandy began to reply then stopped when she noticed Lydia rub a hand over her stomach again. "Are you ill?"

"No." Lydia removed the hand from her middle and used it to fan her face.

Mandy leaned into the desk, resting an elbow on its edge. She raised her eyebrows. "Are you pregnant?"

A corner of Lydia's mouth curved into a smile, but the rest of her face portrayed an apologetic expression. "That would be my professional diagnosis; however, we aren't ready to announce it yet."

Mandy squealed with delight. "Lydia, this is wonderful news! You and Connor have been married over a year—nearly two. No one will be particularly surprised, but everyone will certainly be happy for you. Why are you waiting to announce it? Isn't Connor happy?"

"Connor is thrilled. He wants to run through the village shouting the news to anyone who will listen." Her half smile faded and she tucked her hair behind her ear. "I'm the one who asked for more time."

"Do you think something is wrong?"

"No. In fact, I usually tell my expectant patients this amount of early pregnancy nausea is a good sign." She leaned back in her chair and her hand covered her stomach. "I'm afraid people will be less likely to come to me for help once they know I'm with child. I am not ready to be viewed as feeble."

"You feeble?" Mandy shook her head and chuckled. "I doubt that will happen. Besides, you won't be able to hide it much longer." She touched the folded curtains lying on the desk in front of her and traced an embroidered flower with her fingertip. "The village will be eager to celebrate with you and Connor. Let them have their moment."

"You're right." Lydia nodded then held up a finger. "But first you and Levi must have your moment."

* * *

Levi checked his reflection in the glass cabinet doors on the bookcase in his father's office. He could hear the chatter of Bethany and her friends outside the open office door. The girls' voices echoed as they tied decorative ribbons along the pews and made last-minute adjustments to the arrangements of flowers that filled the chapel with the scent of ceremony. He glanced into the chapel then back at his reflection and straightened the knot on the tie at his neck.

John walked into the office, Bible in hand, and stepped behind his desk. He tidied a stack of books and closed a journal, then he looked at Levi. John held an open palm to the chair on the other side of his desk. "There is still half an hour until noon, son. Have a seat." Levi lowered himself into the leather seat and drummed his fingers in rapid pulses on the arm of the chair. His father sat and folded his hands with the cool control of a man accustomed to handling nervous grooms. "Did the village provide everything you need for your home?"

Levi's throat felt constricted. He put a finger to his necktie's knot and loosened it. "Yes. My—our—house is full. People came by throughout the week with linens and furniture and things for the kitchen. The pantry is overflowing with food. It was all very humbling."

"I am glad to hear it." John studied him for a moment then leaned forward. "Are you and Mandy certain you wish to make that house your home instead of living at our property? You will inherit it one day."

Levi appreciated the new respect John displayed for him. "Yes, Father. We're certain."

"How do you feel about Connor and Lydia moving into the main house, then? They will no doubt have a family of their own soon. Connor says they are satisfied with building onto the cottage, but with so much unused space in the main house it seems unnecessary."

Levi cleared his dry throat. "I think Lydia and Connor should move into the house. Bethany will probably marry as soon as she finishes school, and Aunt Isabella needs Lydia's care. I believe it would be a good arrangement for everyone."

John nodded and scratched his beard. "Excellent. As my heir, I think you should be present when I tell them. They will want to know they have your approval."

"Of course." Levi heard the wedding guests beginning to arrive. He glanced through the open doorway and into the chapel.

John stood and walked to a pitcher of water on a side table near the window. He poured a glass and handed it to Levi. "Your mother would have been proud of you."

Levi only nodded. He quaffed the water in two quick swallows and passed the glass back to his father.

John set the empty glass back on the table and put his hand to Levi's back. "It is time to watch for your bride's arrival."

As Levi walked from the office into the long, open chapel, his eldest sisters came through the front doors. Adeline and Maggie—both flanked by husbands and small children—wore infectious smiles that reminded Levi of his mother. His sisters waved at him as their husbands wrangled the children into a pew. Little Gabe broke free and dashed through the incoming guests.

"Uncle Levi!" The six-year-old wrapped both arms around Levi's dress pants. "You look fancy, Uncle Levi. I caught a frog today."

Levi crouched in front of his nephew and tousled the boy's hair. "That is good news. You can tell me all about it next time I see you. All right?"

"All right," Gabe answered as his mother stood in the aisle and called to him. The little boy glanced up at Levi. "I have to go now. Bye."

Levi rose and smiled as his nephew ran back to Adeline, then he noticed the watching eyes of the growing crowd. To combat the threat of anxiety brought by the attention of the entire village, he only had to think of his bride. He would do anything for her—build a house, stand in front of a crowd, shirk tradition—and soon, vow his love.

As the church's rows filled with guests, he heard a flurry of activity outside the chapel. He stepped near the altar beside his father and fixed his gaze on the chapel's tall front doors. The last of the guests entered with a hurry. The bride had arrived. Levi folded his hands in front of him and exhibited a steadiness that contradicted the shaking in his knees. He took a slow breath and watched as Everett and Roseanna walked into the chapel.

Everett escorted Roseanna to the front row. She winked at Levi as she sat on the pew. Everett sat beside her. Levi looked back to the open chapel doors and tried not to hold his breath.

Backlit by the noon sun, Mandy's silhouette appeared in the doorway. She stepped into the chapel wearing a long, light blue dress, the back of which trailed behind her. A string of white pearls held the blanket of her fiery curls off her face. She held a full bouquet of tiny yellow daisies. Over the sound of his heartbeat, Levi heard the collective gasp of the awestruck crowd. He drew a breath and felt the fluttering in his chest dissipate as his pulse changed to a slow rhythm that matched the pace of her steps while she walked down the aisle with her father.

Levi gazed into her eyes, unconcerned with his own expression, as she gradually moved closer to the altar. A raw mix of pride and humility flowed through his spirit as he watched his bride coming to join her life to his. The image of her in that moment would be the image he saw every time he looked at her for the rest of her life.

Samuel kissed his daughter's cheek and then held her hand out to Levi. He took her hand. Samuel nodded once then turned and sat beside Roseanna.

Levi and Mandy turned and faced the overseer. John read from the scripture, inspiring and admonishing them with the book's wise and ancient instructions for marriage. Then he took a thick piece of grayish paper from between the cover of the Bible and the Old Testament and he cleared his throat. He held his Bible in one hand and kept the paper steady atop it with the other hand. "Levi William Colburn, will you have this woman as thy wedded wife, to live together after God's ordinance in the holy estate of matrimony? Will you love her, comfort her, honor and keep her, in sickness and in health, forsaking all others as long as you both shall live?"

"I will." After he answered the overseer, he glanced at Mandy and saw the slow smile rise on her face.

"Amanda Grace Foster, will you have this man as thy wedded husband, to live together after God's ordinance in the holy estate of matrimony? Will you love him, respect him, obey and keep him, in sickness and in health, forsaking all others as long as you both shall live?"

"I will."

Levi heard the pride in his father's voice throughout the ceremony; still, his gaze remained on his bride. "I, Levi, take you, Amanda, to be my wife, from this day forward, promising to love you faithfully all of my days. With God's help, I will protect you and provide for you and speak kindly to you as long as we both shall live."

Mandy's thin fingers trembled slightly as she pledged her love to him. "I, Amanda, take you, Levi, to be my husband, from this day forward, promising to love you faithfully all of my days. With God's help, I will honor you and comfort you and speak well of you as long as we both shall live."

John pulled a delicate silver band from his breast pocket and handed it to Levi. He felt the smile spread across his face as he slipped it on her finger. His father looked out and addressed the audience. He asked if there were any objections and when there were none, John pronounced them man and wife. Then he looked at Levi. "Son, you may kiss your bride."

As Levi kissed Mandy in front of his father and her parents and the entire village, he lingered long enough to elicit a mix of giggles and cheers from the crowd and one particularly poignant whistle, which came from Connor.

He took her hand and led her away from the altar as the beaming guests rose and applauded. He whisked her through the chapel doors and down the stone steps. Then he opened the door to a topless carriage parked in front of the chapel and she climbed aboard. He sat beside her on the upholstered bench seat then closed the carriage door and rapped his hand on it, signaling the driver to take off.

People poured out of the chapel and tossed grain above the carriage, causing a shower of fertile seed to rain on Levi and Mandy. She laughed and tucked her face into his neck as the carriage escaped the crowd and rattled across the cobblestones, through the village to their new home.

* * *

The morning air in the chilly house nipped at Mandy's exposed toes. She tucked her feet beneath the quilt and nestled close to Levi on the soft, feather bed. Though the bedroom window faced west, the glow of morning light coaxed her eyes open.

She lay still on the bed, trying not to wake her husband, and glanced around the room. Everything in sight was either made by Levi or given to them by village families. She knew who made the quilt that covered them and the curtains that hung over the windows. Through the bedroom's doorway she could see into the front room and part of the kitchen. Sunlight sifted through the sheer curtains on the window above the kitchen sink. She knew the cupboards were filled with dishes and the pantry overflowed with food. The village had supplied everything they could possibly need for a home—their home.

She was still amazed he had built the house with the intention of spending his life there with her. He said he would love her whether she loved him or not. She traced a finger along his bare shoulder. Without a doubt, she loved him.

In time, the growl of her empty stomach lured Mandy out of bed and to the stocked pantry. She grew excited at the thought of going into the kitchen on her first morning as a wife. On her way, she found the starched, white shirt Levi wore to their wedding strewn over the back of a kitchen chair. She pulled the half-buttoned shirt over her head and rolled the sleeves to her wrists as she tiptoed into the kitchen.

On the countertop near the window she found a breadbasket covered with a tea towel. She peeled back the cloth and breathed in the pleasant scent of pastry. She picked up a shiny kettle from the top of the cook stove and carried it to the sink. With her bare foot, she pressed a wooden pedal on the floor beneath the sink. Then she filled the kettle with the water that poured from the faucet. Trying to keep the sounds of the kitchen quiet, she moved in slow increments to find a match, open the firebox, and light the waiting gray leaf chips inside the stove. Then she placed the filled kettle on the stovetop directly over the firebox.

Mandy stepped into the small pantry and inspected its carefully arranged contents. The shelves were lined with packets of spices, sacks of milled grain, and jars of preserves from village gardens. Baskets along the floorboard brimmed with fresh vegetables, berries, and fruits. She reached to a high shelf, shifted a few items, and found a canister marked *Coffee Leaves*.

Opening the canister, she breathed in the dark scent of the fragrant leaves, dried and ready for brewing. As she stepped out of the pantry, she glanced up and saw Levi. He stood at the edge of the kitchen with his shoulder against the wall. He grinned as he watched her prepare breakfast. "Good morning, Mrs. Colburn."

"I like the sound of that." She smiled as she set the canister of coffee on the countertop and picked a silver spoon from a drawer.

Levi inched closer. "I like you in my shirt."

She grinned and flipped her hair over her shoulder then reached to the cupboard. She opened the cupboard door and took down two coffee cups. When she spotted the little smiling face carved on the edge of the cupboard door, she pressed her lips together then pointed to it and glanced at him.

His eyes followed her finger to the carving. "Oh, you were not supposed to see that."

"Why not?" Mandy smiled, knowing the answer. She pulled a curl of hair through her fingertips as Levi's hands came around her waist.

"Because the woman who carved it told me one day my wife might see it and become jealous."

Mandy thought back to the day she spent working with Levi in the house and realized she was now living out what she thought then to be impossible. She sighed. "Your wife."

"My wife. Will you ever get used to that?"

"Of course," She answered. "Will you?"

"No." His low voice hummed with contentment. "I will awaken in awe every morning with you beside me."

CHAPTER FIFTEEN

A layer of fresh snow crunched beneath Levi's boots as he walked through the darkened yard to the shed at the edge of the Colburn property. A cold wind blew in from the ocean. It whistled through the thin line of forest between Levi and the shore and forced him to shield his face with the lapel of his woolen coat.

Dim light spilled out of the cracked shed door and ignited blue specks on the snow in Levi's path. He dropped his lapel and pulled the door open. Once inside, he closed the shed door as far as it would go, but a two-inch gap remained.

Connor was sitting on an overturned bucket holding a wire fragment near the lantern. He glanced up. "Are they ready to play cards?"

Levi shook his head. "The girls are still cleaning up from dinner." He knocked the snow from his boots and scanned the piles of debris they had recovered from the fallen satellite months before. "Have you decided what you are going to do with all this?"

Connor selected a razor from the toolbox at his feet, then he began slicing the green plastic around a long wire. "My first thought is: take it to class and give a lecture on space technology, but I have to be careful what I teach here. Since we don't know how the Land remains undetected by the rest of the world, the last thing I want to do is introduce the students to anything they could use to jeopardize their own safety."

"That's not a worry if your students are anything like me when I was in school. My teachers could have talked about space technology all day long and I would still have no idea what to do with a bunch of metal and wires." Levi picked up an empty bucket from the dirt floor. He flipped it over and sat near the light among the piles of cut pipe and bundled wire. He watched as Connor split the charred plastic off several more wires and pulled the lengths of copper from them. "What is your second thought?"

A smile spread across Connor's face. "Since I'm going to have a child soon, I could use it to build a one-of-a-kind mobile to hang over my kid's crib. Maybe I'll whittle a toy fighter jet to hang in the middle."

"I could help with that." Levi chuckled and watched Connor as he stripped another wire. The man he once considered a threatening outsider was now one of his closest friends and his brother-in-law. "Again, congratulations. I'm glad the secret is out. Mandy and I were relieved when Lydia announced it at dinner tonight."

"Connor? Levi?" The door creaked open and both men looked up as Everett stepped into the shed. He shivered and rubbed his gloved hands together.

When the lantern light hit Everett's face, Levi could see his nose and cheeks were red from walking to the Colburn property in the cold wind. Levi stood. "We missed you at dinner. Is your father feeling better?"

Connor stopped stripping wire and looked up. "What's wrong with Samuel?"

"He stayed in bed all day." Everett closed the door and turned to tug on it again when it didn't close all the way. "He says it's his joints, but my mother is too worried for that to be all."

"Does Lydia need to go see him?" Connor asked, concern marking his brow.

Everett shook his head. "He refuses medicine. He says Doctor Ashton couldn't help him with his ailment when he was young, so he does not want to trouble another doctor."

Levi thought of the amount of work Everett had to do running the farm by himself. "If you need help tomorrow, let me know."

Everett nodded. "Thank you. Tonight my father told me it's time to hire a farmhand. Mrs. Vestal has been asking about work for her nephew, Nicholas. I will pass the message through Bethany." Everett looked at the bundle of wires in Connor's hand. "Have you repurposed the solar panels yet?"

Levi lifted his hands in resignation. "You amaze me, Everett. You're a sheep farmer—how do you understand all this?"

"He understands because he was in my class last year." Connor grinned and set the razor back in the toolbox then looped the bundles of harvested wire into a circle, tucking the spiny ends under. He

246 • KEELY BROOKE KEITH

dropped the wire bundle on a heap of others and brushed his hands together. "Although I don't recall mentioning solar technology last year."

Everett smiled and shook his head. "You didn't. I may not be in school anymore, but Bethany is and she tells me everything."

Connor looked at Levi with his eyes widened and pointed at Everett. "Are you going to take that? You gave me grief when you found out I was in love with Lydia. You know this guy is in love with Bethany, right?"

Levi shrugged. "I can't be mad at Everett if he's in love with my sister."

Connor lifted a palm with incredulity. "And why not?"

"Because I'm married to his sister." Levi grinned.

Everett squared his shoulders and smirked. "Besides, why fight the inevitable?"

Connor leaned his elbows onto his knees and looked at Everett. "Don't get too cocky—half of the guys in Bethany's class are in love with her, too."

Everett's grin disappeared. "Are they prepared to fight for her?"

"Bethany knows you are what's best for her, Everett." Levi realized he had no real evidence for his assumption, but he didn't want Everett riled up. "And if she forgets, I'll remind her."

Connor chuckled. "In my experience, the surest way to get a Colburn to resist you is to say you know what's best for them."

Levi could think of several examples confirming Connor's observation. Regardless, if his baby sister was going to marry anyone, Levi wanted it to be Everett Foster. "Bethany is different from Lydia and me. She is... naïve. Everett knows how to take care of her."

"I couldn't agree more." Connor stood to leave. "But I suggest you let her come to that conclusion herself."

Levi stepped to the door but kept his head down so as not to make contact with the low ceiling. He gave Everett a hearty smack on the back as he passed. "Let's go play cards, brother."

* * *

Levi filed behind the two other men as they approached the main house. When his foot crossed the threshold, he felt the cold wind at his back and the warmth from the gray leaf log burning in the fireplace inside. He closed the door and leaned his hand against it while he wiped his boots on the mat. Then he looked at his wife. Mandy dried a dinner plate and handed it to Bethany, who was stacking dishes in the cupboard. The women giggled as they whispered to each other, and he briefly wondered if Bethany was getting a womanly education.

Levi shrugged out of his coat and hung it on a hook on the wall as he watched Mandy walked to the sink. She glanced at him and curved her lips in a playful smile as she pulled the dishtowel through her fingers. He grabbed the towel out of her hands, tossed it to the sink, and pulled her into a kiss.

"Whoa—haven't you two got a house to do that in?" Connor mocked embarrassment at their display of affection as he stepped to the kitchen table and dropped a deck of cards onto its surface.

Everett feigned a scowl and took a seat at the head of the table. "That's my sister he is manhandling." He laid a bag of wooden marbles by the oil lamp in the center of the table. Mandy rolled her eyes at Everett's comment.

Lydia grinned as she carried a stack of small bowls to the table. "Let them be. I think it's sweet— they've only been married two months." She set one bowl on the table in front of each player then sat beside Connor. He put his arm over the back of her chair.

"Thank you, Lydia." Levi followed Mandy as she sauntered to the table.

Bethany sat at the opposite end of the table from Everett and curled her long legs beneath her in the chair. "May I play too?"

Levi nodded at her then sat at the table. He heard his father speaking to Isabella in the parlor. John came through the doorway into the kitchen. Looking at his father, Levi motioned to the game being spread on table. "Join us for a round, Father."

John stopped near the table and surveyed the game. He put both hands on Levi's shoulders. "Thank you, but I have some reading to do." He gave Levi's shoulders a squeeze then went to the sink and filled a glass with water before returning to the parlor.

Connor picked up the card deck and began to shuffle. As the thick paper cards swished together between his hands, Connor turned to Bethany. "So, you think you're ready to play with the big kids, huh?"

Isabella—still in the parlor—cleared her throat. "You all play fair with my Bethany."

Everyone looked at Bethany and her eyes grew wide. She glanced at their faces then lifted her chin. "It's just a game of bluff. I play it with my friends all the time. How different could it be to play with you?"

Mandy leaned close to Bethany. "Connor taught us to play bluff by adding a draw, so it isn't a simple game of chance anymore. You have to know the possible winning hands in the deck and consider your odds. And right when you think you have it figured out—the other players will try to bluff you."

"Fine. I'm ready." Bethany shifted her feet to the floor and sat up straight. She was doing her best to appear mature—even Levi was almost convinced.

Connor began to deal the cards and glanced at Everett. "All right—she says she's ready."

Bethany made a face at Connor then her eyes moved to Everett. While Connor dealt the cards, Everett and Bethany smiled at each other. Mandy nudged Levi beneath the table and he knew she noticed them, too. Levi enjoyed the new ability to understand Mandy's steady conveyance of nonverbal messages; he considered it one of the many gifts of marriage.

One at a time, the cards flew from Connor's hands into small piles in front of each player. "Full deck with a draw."

Levi examined the cards he was dealt then held them close to his body as he studied the other players. Lydia appeared to be doing math in her head. She dropped two cards to the table. Connor dealt her two more and looked at Bethany. Levi almost instructed her to stop smiling at her cards but decided she would have to learn how to conceal her emotions on her own.

Levi watched Mandy before it was her turn. She had one eyebrow arched a degree and her chin was slightly elevated as she looked at her cards. When Connor turned his attention to her, she dropped her chin and blinked sheepishly. Levi saw her mouth moving as she asked for one card, but her timidity was a ruse. She glanced up at him when it was his turn. Levi left his expression blank and dropped three cards in front of Connor. Connor sifted three new cards from the deck then turned his face toward Everett.

Everett glanced at the cards in his hand and then grinned at Bethany. His dark hair swooped down over his forehead. He gave his head a small jerk to the side sending the hair away from his face. "I like my cards, thank you."

"Great. The dealer takes two." Connor dealt himself two cards. "Who's in?"

"I fold," Lydia said as she laid her cards on the table. Her empty hand immediately covered her belly.

Levi controlled his countenance as he studied each player. One at a time, they took the wooden marbles from the bowl in front of them and dropped the pieces into the pot in the center of the table. Bethany bit her lip and said she was in. Mandy expressed no emotion as she added her pieces to the pot. Levi's cards could easily be beaten, but he stayed in the game anyway. Everett smiled at Bethany as he placed his bet and sent all eyes to her end of the table, taking the focus off himself.

"The dealer is in." Connor matched, exuding his usual unflinching confidence.

Levi watched Bethany. He could tell she believed the outward pretenses, not understanding the true intentions of the players. He wanted to spare her the deception, even though it was only a game. Bethany looked intimidated and folded. After the cards were revealed, she protested the unfairness of the game.

Levi gathered her discarded play from the table and held up her four queens. "This is proof you must learn how to discern a man's bluff and, more importantly, how to control your expressions."

Mandy pulled a long curl through her fingertips. "You brother is right, Bethany. If you learn to control your expressions you will have an advantage. In fact, I once heard that reading a man's bluff requires skill, but—" Mandy turned to Levi and flashed a wicked grin. "—attempting to gauge a woman's bluff requires clairvoyance."

EPILOGUE

J ustin Mercer glanced up from the technical manual he was reading as Volt moved through the narrow doorway and onto the bridge of the icebreaker. Volt carried a dusty portable disc player in one hand and a cluster of archaic compact discs in the other. He held it all up and grinned. "Look at the treasures I found in one of the cabins."

Mercer watched him insert the plug into an electrical outlet behind the chart table. Volt slipped a shiny vintage disc into the player and touched a button. The blaring sound of rock music filled the bridge of the nuclear-powered ship. Volt drew his lips into his mouth and mimed a guitar solo.

Mercer shook his head, dismissing Volt's animation, and stood from the plush leather chair where he had spent hours reading about ship operations. He stretched his neck deeply to one side then to the other. The motion produced a pleasurable popping sound in both directions. He stepped to the front window while holding the thick technical manual in the crook of his arm. Looking down at the open sea, he watched the white caps of the waves disappear as the purloined icebreaker plowed through the liquid tundra. The gray of the austral winter sky in the middle of the South Atlantic was only a minute shade lighter than the gray of the endless ocean. The unchanging light outside the icebreaker signified neither morning nor afternoon, but only day. He checked his wristwatch—still set to Falkland Island Time—to confirm his suspicion that he had indeed been reading all day. Soon the long night would begin.

He looked away from the white caps on the ocean below and glanced at Volt, who was bobbing his head to the beat of the music as he checked the readings on a control panel. After only three days out of port, Mercer knew every instrument on the bridge of the ship and was sure he could handle the operations by himself, but he preferred leaving the work to Volt while he focused on memorizing the rest of the ship's maintenance procedures.

Mercer carried the thick book he had finished reading to a stack of technical manuals piled on the floor. He exchanged it for the manual that included electrical engineering specifications, then he reached to the music player on the chart table and touched a knob, decreasing the music's volume. "I don't know how you can think with that noise."

Volt gave a quick glance back at him and moved to another instrument panel. He drew a notebook from his back pocket and a pencil from behind his ear, then he began writing notes. The ship's radar display blinked and caught Mercer's eye. Both men stepped close to the screen to check it.

Volt pressed a button to reset the display. "It was just a glitch."

"Are you sure?"

"Yeah, mate. No one is even looking for us." Volt went back to his notes. "There's nothing to worry about."

Mercer disagreed—he could think of plenty of things to worry about. He worried they would be chased down by the Royal Navy before he made it to the uncharted land. He worried they would be pirated by some rogue group desperate for supplies. He worried the lack of communications to the Southern Hemisphere only made them believe there was no military activity, lulling them into a false sense of peace, and they could be caught in crossfire. And—considering Volt's notorious career—he worried there could be an enemy on the high seas bent on revenge.

He watched Volt scribble instrument readings into the little notebook. The man was adept at smothering every possible concern Mercer voiced, which only made him more inclined to voice them. It had been a long time since Mercer had met anyone who provided him with any kind of reassurance, and he found himself thirsty for verbal comfort regardless of topic. "We may have made it out of Port Stanley without being noticed, but I don't want to bump into anyone else out here—unless it's a boat full of beautiful women."

Volt tapped on the radar display screen. "Look, nothing but blue from here to Cape Town."

"We're not heading to Cape Town." Mercer envisioned the uncharted land located at the coordinates they were mere days from approaching.

"Anyway, you're wrong. There is something out there."

"Yeah, yeah, your land." Volt laughed and then lowered his volume as the song on the music player ended. "Right, can't forget about your land—green trees, limpid blue waterways and all that."

The sound of a cough came from one of the crewmen downstairs and echoed in the hallway outside the bridge. Mercer stepped back and closed the wood-paneled door. "I thought we left that plague in Port Stanley."

"He's not sick." Volt was quick to reply. "At least we better hope he's not sick—he's the only electrical engineer we've got."

Mercer sat back down in one of the two leather chairs on the bridge and held up the technical manual. "That's why I'm doing my homework."

Volt nodded and plunked down in the other chair. He slid his hands along the leather arms of the chair until his fingers curled around their ends. When his hands were still, his leg began to bounce at the knee. He wouldn't sit for long. Within seconds, Volt shot up and went back to the ship's navigation system.

The sound of coughing echoed again outside the bridge's closed door. Mercer noticed the black of night as it cloaked the windows. He opened the cover of the technical manual and began to read.

Thank you for reading my book. I'm so glad you went on this journey with me. More Uncharted stories await you! Are you ready for the adventure?

I know it's important for you to enjoy these wholesome, inspirational stories in your favorite format, so I've made sure all of my books are available in ebook, paperback, and large print versions.

Below is a quick description of each story so that you can determine which books to order next...

The Uncharted Series
A hidden land settled by peaceful people ~ The first outsider in 160 years

The Land Uncharted (#1)
Lydia's secluded society is at risk when an injured fighter pilot's parachute carries him to her hidden land.

Uncharted Redemption (#2)
When vivacious Mandy is forced to depend on strong, silent Levi, she must learn to accept tender love from the one man who truly knows her.

Uncharted Inheritance (#3)
Bethany and Everett belong together, but when a mysterious man arrives in the Land, everything changes.

Christmas with the Colburns (#4)
When Lydia faces a gloomy holiday in the Colburn house, an unexpected gift brightens her favorite season.

Uncharted Hope (#5)
While Sophia and Nicholas wrestle with love and faith, a stunning discovery outside the Land changes everything.

Uncharted Journey (#6)
When horse trainer Solo moves to Falls Creek, widow Eva gets a second chance at love. Meanwhile, Bailey's quest to reach the Land costs her everything.

Uncharted Destiny (#7)
The Uncharted story continues when Bailey and Revel face an impossible rescue mission in the Land's treacherous mountains.

Uncharted Promises (#8)
When Sybil and Isaac get snowed in, it takes more than warm meals and cozy fireplaces to help them find love at the Inn at Falls Creek.

Uncharted Freedom (#9)
When Naomi takes the housekeeping job at The Inn at Falls Creek to hide from one past, another finds her.

Uncharted Courage (#10)

With the survival of the Land at stake and their hearts on the line, Bailey and Revel must find the courage to love.

The Uncharted Beginnings Series
Embark on an unforgettable 1860s journey with the Founders as they discover the Land.

Aboard Providence (#1)
When Marian and Jonah's ship gets marooned on a mysterious uncharted island, they must build a settlement to survive. Love and adventure await!

Above Rubies (#2)
When schoolteacher Olivia needs the settlement elders' approval, she must hide her dyslexia from everyone, even charming carpenter Gabe.

All Things Beautiful (#3)
Henry is the last person Hannah wants reading her story… and the first person to awaken her heart.

Find out more on my website keelybrookekeith.com or feel free to email me at keely@keelykeith.com where I answer every message personally.

See you in the Land!
Keely

ABOUT KEELY BROOKE KEITH

Keely Brooke Keith writes inspirational frontier-style fiction with a futuristic twist, including *The Land Uncharted* (Shelf Unbound Notable Romance 2015) and *Aboard Providence* (2017 INSPY Awards Longlist).

Born in St. Joseph, Missouri, Keely was a tree-climbing, baseball-loving 80s kid. She grew up in a family who moved often, which fueled her dreams of faraway lands. When she isn't writing, Keely enjoys teaching home school lessons and playing bass guitar. Keely, her husband, and their daughter live on a hilltop south of Nashville, Tennessee.

ACKNOWLEDGEMENTS

Thank you, Marty, for loving me in such a way that I could create one hundred valiant heroes and still have inspiration left over.

Thank you, Rachel, for getting up early in the morning and quietly writing your stories on Daddy's computer while I write mine.

Thank you to those who read early drafts of this story: Pam Heckman, Rod Heckman, Karen Lawler, Amber Barron, Christina Yother, and Annalise Hulsey. Your feedback is invaluable.

CPSIA information can be obtained
at www.ICGtesting.com
Printed in the USA
LVHW112319210322
713955LV00021B/213

9 780692 298626